The Charlie Bell Sting

By

Terry L. Shaffer

ACKNOWLEDGEMENTS

No one can write a book alone. Just as "no man is an island" there are other people behind the scenes who, one way or another, have contributed to the birth of this work. They all deserve my undying gratitude and approbation for their efforts and contributions that made this book possible.

First and foremost is Barbara and Len Eaton, for their staunch support and never-flagging interest and willingness to critique my efforts.

To Becky Geroux whose keen eye missed very little and whose input made such a difference.

To Colleen Bretches, whose grasp of the broad perspective was invaluable.

To David Graves, who added a writer's touch and a large dose of realism.

To Jean Batchelder, who sallied forth until her cataracts made her stop.

Thanks you guys, but for you, this would have remained wishful thinking.

CHAPTER 1

"Bulldog One One Seven declaring an emergency," blared a tense, but carefully modulated masculine voice over the emergency frequency of the Davis-Monthan Air Force Base (Tucson, Arizona) Air Traffic Control network. "I have a double engine compressor stall, I have no flight control and I am too low to attempt a restart. Mayday! Mayday! I am ejecting over the Growler Mountains west of Ajo (Arizona)."

"Tower acknowledges Bulldog One One Seven's emergency at 1640 hours, SAR (search and rescue) units are being alerted," replied a dispassionate female voice.

Captain Greg Miller's heart rate belied his calm voice as he reported his emergency, and panic bubbled near the surface, but he took in a deep breath and donned his training like a sturdy jacket. He tucked his legs in, cinched down hard on his safety harness and pulled the ejection levers on either side of his seat.

Pulling on the levers triggered explosive bolts immediately that jettisoned the aircraft's canopy. Seconds later rocket motors propelled the pilot straight up out of the cockpit. A second later the slipstream caught him as his drogue chute began to deploy his main parachute and the ejection seat chassis fell away. He was dragged backward almost horizontally as his main parachute deployed and blossomed into a huge red canopy. As his aircraft flew on, the slipstream subsided and Captain Miller swung back to nearly a vertical attitude.

Suddenly the silence of no wind and no jet engines was deafening as he tried to maneuver his chute so he could watch his aircraft proceed pilotless toward three thousand-foot-high Growler Peak. Miraculously the A-10 missed the shoulder of the peak seemingly by inches and disappeared below the north side of the mountain. Seconds later, a massive explosion's shock wave sent the pilot nearly horizontal again as he fought for control of his chute. An enormous plume of black smoke roiled skyward beyond the peak, quickly carried to the east by the strong west wind.

Below him, Miller could see that he was drifting away from the valley floor into a rugged canyon and the strong wind hampered his efforts to steer his chute toward what appeared to be a reasonably level landing zone. As he neared the boulder-strewn canyon floor he tried to tuck his legs beneath him to avoid the sharp crags rising up around him. His right knee smashed into a rocky outcrop that tore at his flight suit as he scraped his way down the outcrop and landed on the uneven surface. He immediately unbuckled the safety harness holding him securely in his seat and his knee collapsed beneath him as Miller attempted to gather in his chutes. The wind was strong enough that it kept tearing them loose from his grasp and they dragged him, off-balance, farther into the narrow canyon. Since he couldn't stand up or even rise up on his right knee, he finally resorted to lying on the main chute and gathering it in under his chest.

After collecting the chutes beneath him, Captain Miller lay panting, exhausted from the frantic exertion and in a great deal of pain from his injured knee. The sun seemed to sink early in the desert in autumn and it was nearly full dark before he raised his head and examined his surroundings. The pain in his knee was excruciating and the rest of him felt scraped and banged up after ejecting then colliding with the outcrop. He knew he had to find some sort of shelter. It was the Sonora Desert, after all, and no matter how warm it got during the day, in October, it cooled off quickly at night and, without a moon, such as this evening, the darkness would be complete.

He was lying on a slope heavily littered with rocks and spiny desert cactus. He could see a rocky overhang about ten yards above him with what looked like an indentation below that might offer him some shelter – if he could crawl up to it. He couldn't put any weight on his knee and would have to worm his way up the rocky slope on his left slide.   Dragging his parachute behind him, Miller was grateful the distance was only thirty feet instead of thirty yards as he scooted and wiggled his way up the incline through dust, dirt, sharp rocks and spiny cactus thorns.

Once again he was badly winded by the time he reached the overhang. He hesitated at the rim, wary that other desert fauna, such as a big diamondback, might be using the ledge. He drew a small penlight he used for checking his knee board from a chest pocket, and slowly played the narrow beam around the darkness below the overhang.   It looked more like a shallow cave than just an indentation, and it appeared unoccupied. The best things about it (so far) was that it blocked most of the wind and there was no snake! He squirmed over the ledge onto relatively flat, rocky ground.

The pilot rested for several minutes, and directed his tiny beam into the deeper recesses of the cave. There was a small rock fire ring about four feet back from the edge of the rim and primitive carvings scratched close together on the smooth sections of the walls. He noted that it was less rocky toward the back and assumed that whoever had passed time here before had moved some of the rocks out to make a more comfortable bed in the sand and fine dirt. He dragged his nylon parachute farther into the cave where the wind wouldn't blow it away.

Once his breathing returned to near normal, Miller reached for his emergency radio in his right knee pocket. He had to let his wing man know he was alive and what kind of shape he was in. Unknown to him at the time, his emergency radio had been crushed by the impact with the crag. As he gingerly pulled open the Velcro-flap covering the knee pocket, he winced as the fabric rubbed against his by now rapidly swelling knee. He paused to let the pain subside, then reached into the pocket and was dismayed to find the radio in several pieces.   He extracted the largest and saw that the all-important radio was smashed beyond repair.

His concern about his situation ratcheted up, but he didn't

panic; he was too well trained for that. He knew a SAR mission would be launched and he'd just have to wait and make his presence known when the searchers were nearby.

Miller set about digging a bowl in the floor at the rear part of the cave for a bed. As he dug and smoothed out his bed, Miller wished he had his survival pack from the bottom of his seat. He knew there were several pints of water among the other gear in the pack and he was thirsty. He also hoped fervently that his locator beacon had activated as it was supposed to when he ejected. So far he had not heard any other aircraft in the area, which surprised him. His wing man, First Lieutenant Jesse Grimes, should have had enough time and fuel to turn around from his return to Davis-Monthan and attempt to locate him. It was a little early for a SAR helo, and Miller wondered if they would try to locate him but not attempt a rescue in the dark due to the rugged terrain. The locator beacon would at least let them know he got out of the aircraft okay, and where he was.

He was in the process of scooping a handful of dirty sand into the bottom of his bed when his hand struck something solid that didn't move and didn't feel like a rock. He dug down a little deeper around the object, finding a rounded corner.

He turned on his penlight, which he had turned off when he started digging to save the battery, and found what looked to be the corner of a valise or something similar. It was of aged, flaking leather, badly discolored and Miller still couldn't get it to budge. He turned off his light, and began digging around the edges in earnest. The side he was excavating was about three inches thick and spanned at least a foot before turning ninety degrees. The shape became a rectangular object as he uncovered it, until it narrowed down to just the width of a single layer of leather.

He could wiggle what he had uncovered a little but couldn't dislodge it with what leverage he could muster laying on his side. The digging continued until the pilot had uncovered the entire outline of the object. He brushed the dirt and sand off, then used the flashlight again and discovered he had unearthed aged saddlebags. The two pouches were not empty. Just then his light started to flicker and moments later went out. His only source of illumination was gone until he recovered his survival pack. He would have to wait until morning to explore the contents of the saddlebags.

He wrapped himself up in the parachute, left his helmet on and fell into an exhausted sleep, his thoughts ratcheting back and forth between being rescued, and wondering about the contents of the saddlebag.

*****

"Bulldog One Two One," called First Lieutenant Grimes, Captain Miller's wingman, and long time friend.

"Go ahead Bulldog One Two One," responded the Davis-Monthan tower.

"I am orbiting the Growler Mountains at this time. I have located Bulldog One One Seven's wreckage north of Growler Peak. I have no night vision capability. I can detect neither signs of a parachute nor the aircraft's canopy. I have fuel enough to orbit for thirty minutes."

"Bulldog One Two One, remain on station as long as possible, then RTB (return to base)."

"Copy that; I'll keep looking but I don't see any lights or hear any beacon on the emergency channel. It's too dark to see a parachute or the cockpit canopy."

"Roger. Bulldog One Two One, remain on site until the SAR helo arrives, fuel permitting."

"Bulldog One Two One, wilco."

Instead of race track formations over the mountains as prescribed, Bulldog One Two One began flying nap of the earth maneuvers with landing lights on, backtracking from the crash site in hopes of spotting any clue to Bulldog One One Seven's

11

whereabouts. Nap of the earth maneuvers consisted of flight barely above the ground, following the terrain.

On a genuine combat mission where the aircraft was armed with AGM-65 Maverick missiles, the pilot would have had infrared targeting capabilities. Had the mission included night maneuvers, the pilot would have been equipped with night vision equipment but not during a daylight sortie.

The 46th Rescue Wing HH-60G Pave Hawk helicopter arrived just as Bulldog One Two One was about to announce his departure from the site of the crash. "Pedro Sixty-Six to Bulldog One Two One," came a deep masculine voice over the common frequency.

"Bulldog One Two One."

"Have you seen any wreckage besides that of the aircraft itself?"

"That's negative, I have zero night vision capability; I've been orbiting looking for a light or a tone. No joy on either. I'm just about bingo fuel so I'll leave this in your capable hands."

"Bulldog One Two One, thank you for the assist."

The helo flew directly to the aircraft wreckage and found a fairly open space nearby where they could land and disgorge a ground SAR team. Then the Pave Hawk lifted off and began an infrared grid search from the wreckage upstream, vectoring along what little debris trail there was.

The first order of business for the on-scene SAR supervisor was to examine the cockpit area of the burned out aircraft to confirm whether there was an ejection or if there was a body. That was quickly established and communicated to the SAR Coordinator and Pedro Sixty-Six. The "ground pounders" then began back-tracking the debris field in order to establish a more accurate vector for Pedro Sixty-Six's search.

In a perfect world, the ground team would follow the trail of debris and torn up and scorched earth to where the aircraft had first impacted the ground. It would be a relatively straight line unless the aircraft collided with something during its final moments of motion. If the ground crew continued along that line, and they were lucky, they would find the ejection seat's chassis and some indication that the pilot had landed safely or otherwise. They would factor in wind drift, considering the strong wind still blowing and, hopefully, come up with a pilot. No infrared sign of him was puzzling. Surely no one had preceded them and picked him up?

Ninety minutes later Pedro Sixty-Six reported finding the ejection seat chassis on the Growler Valley floor about six miles south of the crash site. The location of the chassis gave the search team another vector point and, after allowing for the wind drift, they adjusted the path of their search.

Captain Miller was oblivious to this activity, mercifully sleeping despite the pain from his knee injury.

CHAPTER 2

Greg Miller woke up with a jolt, as a fearsome pain ripped through his right knee. He had started to roll over and an excruciating awakening was his reward. Next came thirst. It reminded him of where he was and what his circumstances were. Thirst competed with pain for primacy.

It occurred to him that he could dimly see inside the cave - the sun was coming up. He lay there staring at the tapering ceiling of rock three feet above his head and decided that if he didn't find water he would die. The knee pain might feel like he was dying but he knew the thirst would kill him. He thought of his survival pack just down the hill with his ejection seat. There was water in the survival pack. He decided he had to brave the pain to drink, and the only thing holding him back was his fear of the pain. He thought it ludicrous that he would die of thirst thirty feet from water because his knee hurt.

He rolled over on his left side and began unwrapping himself from his parachute. The chute and its shrouds were in a snarl and he was more tangled up in the shrouds than he liked but the damned thing had kept him warm. As he struggled painfully to untangle himself from the parachute, his eyes fell on the saddlebag. *No, I need water first,* his parched throat told him.

He finally extricated himself from the parachute and, again on his left side, began squirming and scrabbling his way back down the incline to his ejection seat. It was getting lighter by the minute and the newly risen sun was already beginning to warm the air. It seemed a little easier going downhill but the pain in his knee had not lessened and he could see that the swelling had stretched his baggy flight suit tight near the injured joint. But he was getting closer to water!

At last Miller reached the survival pack and eagerly opened it. Almost desperately he extracted one of the plastic bottles of water. He cracked the lid and drank greedily – until the bottle was empty. He reached for another bottle, opened it and wanted to drink it as fast but forced himself to drink more slowly. Water doesn't do much good if it comes back up because you drink too much too fast.

After finishing off the second bottle, he thought about a third, then started thinking about conserving the rest. After all, he didn't know how much longer he'd be out here and still hadn't heard the sound of any aircraft overhead.

He checked the locator beacon and found that it was *dead.* Non-functioning locator beacons had been a persistent problem since before Captain Miller started flying A-10s. No one knew where he was or if he was even alive! He was glad he hadn't known that last night. His mind kicked more into survival mode and he started thinking ahead, toward what he must now do to stay alive until someone found him. He had a flare gun and a smoke canister in the survival pack in case he heard or saw someone. Right now, he needed to get back to his shelter before the rising sun started to cook him. Laboriously he crawled back to his aerie, this time dragging the survival pack behind him.

It wasn't any easier making his way back to the cave than it had been the first time but, with frequent rests, he made it. He decided to drink one more bottle of water and use it to chase down some of the analgesic tablets from the first aid kit. He then tore open one of the MRE (Meals Ready to Eat) packets and consumed everything edible.

He began to think about how he could signal for help. First thing he needed was someone to signal *to.* He had a signal mirror in the pack but thought smoke during the day and flares at night would be better options. Feeling much better, both physically and emotionally, he relaxed a notch. It was full sunlight now and his attention was once again drawn to the saddlebags. He crawled over to his parachute bed and reached for it. It didn't even occur to him until later to lay the bright red parachute outside as a signal.

One side pouch of the saddlebags clearly had more bulk than the other so he opened that one first. He untied the leather thong that kept the cracked leather cover over the bag, turned it away from him and shook it to evict any critters. Nothing came out so he looked inside. Clothes: A pair of Levis, a blue gingham snap-button long-sleeved western shirt, a pair of socks, a pair of skivvies and a poncho. They seemed to be in reasonably good condition; he had no way of knowing how long the saddlebags had lain buried in the recesses of the cave. Miller looked once again into the open pouch but found nothing else.

He turned to the other one. It too was tied with a leather thong and he hastily untied it, the leather crackling as he opened the cover. He shook the bag as he had done with the first one. Again, no residents emerged. He looked inside and saw a wallet, a book, a small pouch with a long leather thong drawstring and a few sheets of paper. He opened the wallet but found no identification, only twenty-seven dollars in old silver certificates. The book was a small Bible with no name or inscription in it. He jiggled the pouch which was surprisingly heavy for its size, then opened it and spilled out a gold nugget about the size of the first knuckle of his thumb. At least he thought it was gold judging by the weight and color. The surface of the nugget was irregular and looked like it had been molten at some time in the past.

The pilot stared at the nugget for several seconds, his mind going many miles an hour. Then he shrugged, looped the thong over his head and draped the pouch down his collar under the front of his flight suit.

He then reached for the papers. One was an envelope addressed to Jake Humbertson c/o Assayer's Office, Yuma, Arizona Territory. It had been opened and the letter read:

May 12, 1889

Dear Jake,

Josiah and Micah are dead, kilt by a war party of Injuns four days after you left. I was too busy shooting to see what tribe they was from but I suspect a war party of hot-headed local Apaches.

They shot me too but not before I got a couple a the bastards. Lucky for me, an Army patrol rode up and drove the Injuns off. They're tending ta me as best they can. We'll probably stay here at the claim, since they don't want to move me until I'm better – which is doubtful. One of the troopers is riding to Yuma to report the fight and will deliver this letter.

I didn't much like asking you to ride all the way to Yuma to file our claim but now I'm glad I did. Getting it filed was damned important and we just couldn't wait much longer considering all the gold we found. I wasn't too worried about the assay but it made sense to have it done since you were going to be there anyway. So you know, when the redskins started raising hell, we stashed our supplies and equipment, except for some food, the guns, and ammo, in the usual place so the bastards wouldn't steal it.

You take care coming back and God willing, I'll see you then.

Your friend,
Albert Neal

Captain Miller was thunderstruck. 1889? A gold claim? He momentarily forgot his pain until he moved to reach for the next item. It was a receipt dated May 20, 1889, for the filing of a mining claim for the Cactus Wren Claim in the Arizona Territory. The receipt listed claimants of Albert Neal, Josiah Carter, Micah Clapton, and Jake Humbertson. The metes and bounds description of the location was disappointingly vague, "From the tinaja (natural cistern) located at the base of Ahren's Seep, five hunnerd feet northwest to a large boulder with pictures scratched in it, the biggest

17

is a sun symbol. From the sun boulder, two hunnerd fifty feet northeast to another boulder, this one with a scratched-in image just of a snake. From the snake boulder five hunnerd feet southeast to the edge of a wash with a mesquite tree leaning into it. From the mesquite tree two hunnerd fifty feet back to Ahren's Seep.

The next paper was a certificate of assay in Jake Humbertson's name for forty-two ounces of eighty-nine percent pure gold. Also listed was a two-point-two ounce gold nugget that had tested at eighty-seven percent pure.

The final paper was a receipt for forty-two ounces of gold at $20.67 an ounce, dated the same as the claim receipt, issued by the Yuma Bank and Trust. Miller wondered if it was still there after all these years. He would have to check to see if the bank was still in business or if it had merged with another financial institution. And he would have to look up Ahren's Seep when . . .

His attention was drawn away from the papers by the loud thwackaty thwackaty of a helicopter. Frantically, he folded the old papers and tucked them into one of his flight suit's inner pockets. He crawled painfully out of the cave into the bright sunlight, grabbing the smoke grenade and dragging the parachute with him. He couldn't see the helo but it was close. Pushing back the pain from his knee, he spread the chute out as widely as he could then popped the smoke bomb and tossed it a little way down the hill, away from him. White smoke billowed out of the canister and, as the wind caught it, it billowed toward the east. He could still hear the helo and the sound was getting louder.

Suddenly the Pave Hawk was just *there*. It shredded the smoke and he waved. The helo descended then eased over toward the hillside he was on, until it appeared to be directly above him. A waist door opened and a winch boom was rigged out. A Pararescueman appeared and began to descend on the cable being lowered from the aircraft.

The Pararescueman landed lightly and the hook he rode

down ascended a few feet. The man, unidentifiable through his helmet, leaned over Miller and raised his visor. The young man didn't look old enough to vote, but Captain Miller wasn't complaining.

"Are you injured, Sir?" the pararescueman yelled over the whine of the helo's turbines.

Miller nodded and pointed to his hideously swollen right knee. The young man nodded and spoke into his helmet-mounted microphone. The cable was winched back into the helo but moments later was on its way back down with a Stokes stretcher connected. The young man grabbed it to keep it from swinging into his patient, and he laid it flat on the uneven ground next to Miller so the pilot, with the Pararescueman's help, could squirm his way into it. Once that was accomplished, the Pararescueman strapped him in, then said something into his microphone. The slack was taken up in the cable and the stretcher began to rise. As it neared the waist door of the helo, another crewman appeared, steadied the stretcher and hauled Captain Miller aboard.

The crewman unhooked the stretcher and made the cable ready to lower again. As it began to descend, he turned to his patient and secured the Stokes to the deck. He began checking Miller's vital signs and thoroughly examined him for other injuries. Meanwhile the first Pararescueman came aboard, secured the winch assembly and stowed the boom. He removed Captain Miller's helmet and placed a set of headphones over his ears. Captain Miller could now hear the conversation in the cabin, the noise was appreciably reduced.

"Captain," the second crewman asked, "are we leaving anything on the ground you think we should recover?"

"Just the survival pack," said Captain Miller, grimacing, his knee was hurting badly due to the jostling it had undergone getting into the helo.

"Already got that, Sir; anything else?"

"Can you give me something for the pain? My knee is

killing me."

"Let me just do some quick checks first." He pulled out a small penlight and shone it toward Captain Miller's eyes.

"Any dizziness or nausea?" the young crewman asked.

"No. As far as I can tell I just got bumped around a little except for my knee which crashed into a rock."

"Okay, Sir. Are you allergic to anything?"

The Captain shook his head, whereupon the crewman injected him with morphine after cutting his flight suit sleeve all the way up to the shoulder. Beginning at the pilot's boot he also cut open the flight suit's leg all the way to the waist. He uncovered the injured knee, saw no blood, and immobilized it by strapping it to Captain Miller's other leg. The Pararescueman started a saline solution IV as a hedge against dehydration.

"We're going to take you to St. Joseph's in Tucson, it's a Level 1 Trauma Center. They'll take good care of you there. We're about forty minutes out. Is the morphine starting to kick in?"

Captain Miller only nodded, the drug was making him woozy but he was still alert enough to know that he had to protect the nugget around his neck and the papers under his flight suit.

""Can you do me a big favor?" Captain Miller asked hoarsely.

The man nodded.

"I'm carrying some papers – personal papers – that I don't want lost when I get to the hospital. They're not classified or anything. Can you hold onto them until I can come get them?"

The corpsman stared at him for a moment, then looked around him. No one was close by. "They frown on us doing that, but I've done it before. Sure. I'm Spec 5 Tad Morrison and I'll keep an eye on your stuff until you come for it. Just look me up at the 48th Rescue Squadron."

"The papers are in the left inside front pocket of my flight suit," Captain Miller said, "being strapped in, I obviously can't get at them." The Pararescueman unzipped the front of the Captain's flight suit and found the papers tucked inside the pocket. He retrieved them and, without even glancing at them, sealed them in a plastic personal effects envelope whose seal he awkwardly had Captain Miller initial.

"What about the pouch?" the corpsman asked.

"Uh, that's my lucky nugget. It goes with me everywhere."

"They'll remove it at the hospital."

"Better take that too then." Captain Miller mumbled groggily. He was unable to keep awake any longer and closed his eyes. Sometime later he was vaguely aware that the aircraft had landed and he was being transferred from the Stokes to a hospital gurney. He didn't care, and went back to sleep.

CHAPTER 3

Captain Miller dreamed that he was waking up, but when he opened his eyes in the dream, he was still in the cave and there was no water. He was very thirsty and craved water more than anything. He couldn't move his knee but it didn't hurt! He was grateful for that but he still desperately needed a drink.

Some soft, external sound roused him and he opened his eyes, this time for real – but not for long. He was still under the influence of anesthesia and only semi-conscious. He drowsed in and out of wakefulness. Finally he heard the sharp sound of a door knob turning and opened his eyes. He was surprised to find himself in a hospital bed, on his back with his head raised about a third. His right knee was tightly wrapped and he couldn't feel anything, including the pillow beneath the joint.

A nurse dressed in a flowered smock noticed he was awake and came over to the bed. "Mr. Miller? Can you hear me?" she asked in a loud voice.

"It's time to wake up," she said in a louder tone. She straightened his blankets and repeated, "It's time to wake up."

Miller turned his head to the right and saw a bed table bearing a small plastic cup that he fervently hoped contained water. Weakly, he reached for the cup but the nurse beat him to it.

"Thirsty, huh? Let me help." She picked up the cup, inserted a straw and held it to his lips. "Take it easy, don't try to drink it all at once, there's plenty more," she murmured.

He drew in a mouthful of room temperature water and swallowed. Surprisingly, the one swallow refreshed his mouth, he wondered why he wasn't more thirsty. The IV in his arm was probably re-hydrating him, he thought.

"More?" she asked and held the cup near his mouth. He

shook his head and she put the cup back on the table.

She began taking his blood pressure and he croaked, "Where am I?"

"You're in St. Josephs Hospital in Tucson. You broke your right kneecap and they had to operate to repair it. You'll be fine."

"Will I still be able to fly?" he asked anxiously.

"I don't know. When I finish here, I'll go find your doctor and let him know you're awake."

The nurse finished her work and quietly left the room. Not twenty minutes later a man in green scrubs tapped on the door then entered. He was about Captain Miller's age, thirty plus or minus a couple of years, medium height with wavy brown hair and brown eyes. As he walked over to the bed, he smiled when he saw Miller was awake.

"I'm Doctor Ballard, your surgeon. How are you feeling?"

"Kinda out of it, you must have had to dope me up pretty good?

Dr. Ballard nodded. "Your knee was really swollen by the time we got to you. As I understand it, it took a while to find you and that, along with no ice, is why it was so swollen. Had we been able to get ice on it right away, it would have been a little simpler surgery but it wasn't anything we hadn't seen before. Your kneecap – your patella – was broken into several pieces and we had to wire and screw them back together. There were some smaller pieces we just couldn't piece back together so we removed them so they wouldn't interfere with the knee's function."

"So I'm okay? Will I be able to fly again?" Miller asked, holding his breath.

"As far as I'm concerned, yes. Your kneecap will mend in about six weeks and then, perhaps after some physical therapy, you should be good to go. But I'm not a flight surgeon mind you; I have no idea what one will say."

"How soon will I be discharged?"

"Due to the swelling, we're a little concerned about blood

clots forming so I'd like to see you stay at least twenty-four hours, maybe longer if the swelling doesn't start to go down."

"I wonder if they'll transfer me to the base hospital now that the surgery is done," Greg mused.

"If I write on your chart that you can probably be released this time tomorrow, I doubt they'd bother."

"Anything I can do to help this along in the right direction?"

"Keep doing the ankle pumps the nurse will show you. They increase blood circulation which keeps the clots from forming and helps reduce the swelling. You're fitter than most, and that will be working for you too. Any other questions?"

"Cast or brace?"

"Due to the swelling, I think we'll fit you with a brace that you can adjust as the swelling goes down." He raised his eyebrows as if to invite any other questions, Miller shook his head and the doctor nodded.

"Thank you, Doctor Ballard, for all you've done for me, I appreciate it."

"That's what I'm here for," he said with a smile, "and thank *you* for doing what you're doing for the country."

Dr. Ballard left and Captain Miller heaved a big sigh of relief.

Six weeks, he mused, *I can get a lot of research done on Jake Humbertson, his friends and the Cactus Wren claim.*

There was another knock on the door and a nurses' aide opened the door with Miller's dinner. He suddenly realized he was famished and waved the young woman into the room. On her heels came his best friend and wingman, First Lieutenant Jesse Grimes. Grimes was slightly younger than Miller, at twenty-eight, but they could have passed for brothers. They were of the same height, five feet nine, and both were broad-shouldered and athletic. Jesse had blue eyes while Greg's were hazel but they both had brown, short hair and fair complexions in handsome faces. The biggest difference between them was that Jesse often spoke with a Texas twang.

The aide slipped out of the room immediately after placing the food tray on the patient's bedside table.

"When I heard y'all was out of surgery I headed over to check on y'all myself. How y'all doin'?"

Greg didn't hesitate to dig right into his food. Jesse asked his question as Greg was taking a bite of his hamburger. He had to chew and swallow the mass before he could answer. "I'm doing okay *now*, twelve hours ago I wouldn't have said that."

"You sure made a mess of Uncle Sam's airplane!" Jesse quipped with a grin.

"It damned near made a big mess out of me," Greg retorted. "I didn't know what to do. I was pulling out of my last strafing run at BMGR (Barry M. Goldwater (bombing) Range and suddenly I had nothing. I was still low, climbing out of the run, and I had no power at all and no flight control. I had begun a re-start sequence when I remembered what they told us over and over, "If you don't think you can solve the problem or do a workaround in time, get out! So I got out.

"The ejection was okay but there was about a twenty-knot wind from the west which blew me out of the Growler Valley and into the mountains. Just before I landed, my knee and my damned radio smashed into a rock outcrop and that's how I got hurt. The doc says I'll be alright but it will be up to a flight surgeon to decide if I can fly and when."

"Your knee, huh?" asked Jesse, nodding toward Greg's heavily bandaged knee.

"Yeah, like my radio, I broke my kneecap into pieces. They had to wire and screw it back together. It'll take about six weeks to heal."

"I never did hear your beacon, and I orbited for half an hour."

"Big surprise, huh? It was pretty lonely out there once I found out I had no way to communicate except flares and smoke. Luckily the smoke did its job. So did the helo's crew, I have to remember to send them a thank you, atta boy letter."

"When do y'all think they'll release you?"

"Doctor Ballard wanted me to stay twenty-four hours. He's concerned about blood clots forming."

"Twenty-four hours? After a surgery like yours? That seems like an awful short period of time after surgery."

"I have a feeling this doctor knows what he's doing. Besides, I don't want to stay here any longer than necessary; I have things that need doing."

"Like what? You're all crippled up."

"That won't be a problem, at least for a while . . . Close the door," Greg said, lowering his voice and looking over Jesse's shoulder at the mostly open door.

Jesse walked over and closed the door.

"Pull up a chair, we need to talk."

Mystified, Jesse skidded a chair over to the side of Greg's bed, sat down, and looked expectantly at his friend.

"I holed up in a shallow cave overnight," Greg began. "It had been used as a shelter long before as there was a fire ring and some petroglyphs scratched into the walls. I dug a shallow bowl in the sand and rocks in the cave for a bed and uncovered some old saddlebags buried way in the back. Besides a few old clothes, I found a gold nugget in a pouch, some papers, and a letter telling about a gold claim somewhere between the Growler Mountains and Yuma."

Greg paused for breath and noticed Jesse was paying close attention. He was glad, this was important.

"Among the other papers was a receipt for a gold mining claim filed by a guy named Jake Humbertson who had three partners back in 1889. There was a letter from one of the partners, Albert Neal, telling Humbertson that while Humbertson had been gone to Yuma to file the claim, he and his partners had been attacked by renegade Indians and the other two partners had been killed. Albert Neal had been wounded. The final papers were an assay report on forty-two ounces of gold and a receipt from a bank for the value of the gold. In those days, gold was only valued at $20.67 an ounce. Considering where I found the saddlebags, I'm guessing the Indians got Humbertson too, but he managed to stash this stuff in the cave and draw the Indians away. The receipt for the mining claim gives only a very vague description of the location of the claim. It seems to me that, with a little luck and a lot of researching, we might find that gold claim." Jesse stared at Greg for over a minute. "Y'all are serious, aren't ya?"

"As an ejection seat, and you *know* how serious I am about those! The certificate of claim was very vague. It said one corner of the claim was a certain distance from a certain rock near Ahren's Seep. If we narrow down where, between Yuma and the Growler Mountains. the seep – a dry bed I assume – is, we might have a shot at finding it, the landmark and the claim."

"Let me see the certificate of claim," said Jesse.

"I can't right this minute. I had to leave the papers and the gold nugget with one of the Pararescuemen in the chopper who is with the 48th Rescue Squadron. He put them in sealed personal property envelopes and said that I could have them whenever I was able to come get them. I figure we can do that tomorrow when I'm released."

"Don't put y'all's cart before the horse. Tomorrow I reckon you won't feel much like dancin'. I'll come by here tomorrow and pick you up and, dependin' on how y'all are feeling, we'll decide if we go to the base or I take you right home. They just hacked up your knee, son, and you're going to hurt for a spell."

"Then we'd better get over there first thing before the nerve block wears off. That should be our first stop after we leave here tomorrow."

"We'll see."

CHAPTER 4

Getting out of the hospital turned out to be almost as arduous an effort as getting rescued. Good as his word, Doctor Ballard signed the release order almost exactly twenty-four hours after Captain Miller was admitted. Then the red tape brigade took over and multiplied due to the military presence in a civilian hospital. Then there were the occupational health therapists who had to teach him how to go up and down stairs with crutches, how to use the toilet and how to get in and out of a car with a knee that wouldn't bend.

Finally, with a sigh of relief, Greg contorted himself into the front seat of Jesse's Highlander, and, at Greg's urging, Jesse headed toward Davis-Monthan Air Force Base and the 48th Rescue Squadron's offices. On the way, at Greg's direction, Jesse stopped at a liquor store and bought a bottle of Jack Daniels Single Barrel Select Tennessee whiskey.

His white face belied his words but Greg insisted he wasn't in pain when they arrived at the 48th Rescue Squadron. On crutches, Greg and Jesse went in search of Sergeant Tad Morrison. They found him quickly and he handed over two envelopes of personal property and Jesse handed over the bottle of "special lubricant" in appreciation.

They made one other stop on the way home - to a pharmacy where Jesse was able to get Greg's pain pill prescription filled. Greg took two of the pills dry before they even got home. When they arrived at their ground floor apartment (thank God), Greg painfully made his way inside, leaving Jesse to bring in what little Greg had carried with him into the hospital and, of course, the papers and nugget from the cave.

Greg collapsed on his side on the couch. Jesse sliced open

the envelope and spilled the papers and the pouch onto the coffee table. Greg just lay there for several minutes while the narcotic took effect and Jesse, meanwhile, went through the papers.

"Y'all awake?" Jesse asked.

"Yeah, just letting the pills take effect."

"Is an 'I told you so,' in order?"

"Shut up."

Jesse grinned. He picked up each piece of paper separately and examined it minutely. "I wonder what became of the gold, if it's still in the bank's custody or if it was auctioned off. And where is that claim? I reckon it has expired by now or someone else took it over."

"That's some of the research I planned on doing," said Greg, shifting uncomfortably on the couch. "I thought I'd start with basic name checks on the four partners to see if they left any family. I'm sure someone would like to know what happened to their ancestor even if there's nothing to inherit. If the gold still exists in the bank, they might stand to inherit it, but I have to believe the gold still on the claim is up for grabs."

"This is a placer gold claim, right?" Jesse asked. Greg nodded. "That means the gold is extracted from gravel or loose material, not hard rock?"

"Yeah, it's panned or in some other way extracted from the material in a stream bed or something similar."

"If we found the claim, what are your thoughts about what to do with it?"

"We work it, of course."

"You mean get all the prospecting equipment and actually pan the claim for gold?"

"Jesse, gold is going for well over $1800 an ounce! That nugget you've been fondling is worth over $3600!"

"Which begs the question, where did it come from?"

"I suppose nuggets can be found in stream beds too, which assumes it was found at or near the claim."

"Okay. Well first things first. I'll start checking on the internet; you take a nap."

Greg didn't argue and in minutes, was snoring. Jesse, meanwhile, retrieved his laptop from the den and set it up along with a printer at the kitchen table. He began searching the names from the documents Greg had found. He quickly discovered that without more specific information such as a date of birth or an idea from where the four partners came he was spitting into the wind. Just trying to find all the people with the same name on Facebook was a daunting task and, based on what Jake Humbertson had written in the letter and on the documents, there was no trail to follow.

The Yuma Bank and Trust could be a more viable lead. At least there was a chance the bank's archives were still available and they which might suggest where the Cactus Wren Claim's gold lay. That would be an in-depth research project beyond Jesse's capability. Finally, Ahren's Seep. Nothing came up on the internet but that didn't mean the creek bed didn't exist. The Bureau of Land Management (BLM) or the U.S. Geological Survey might be places to research an obscure creek bed that had been dry for decades if not centuries.

Jesse had been hunched over his laptop for two and a half hours. He finally sat up straight and stretched. Researching on the internet was not his forte'; he was more of a get-out there-stomp-around-and-find-something type of a guy. Greg was the same way. It was becoming clear that they would have to bring in a researcher to do the fact-finding heavy lifting.

As Jesse sat there staring out the patio door, Greg stirred.

When he groaned, Jesse looked over at him and saw his friend was trying to sit up.

When he saw Jesse looking at him, Greg croaked, "Gotta pee."

"You want some help getting up?" Jesse asked, half rising from his chair.

"Huh uh, I have to learn to do this myself. I'm just glad it's

Saturday and you're around to help me get used to doing things on my own." With another groan and using the arm of the couch, Greg rose and grabbed his crutches. Slowly and awkwardly he hobbled into the bathroom. When he finally returned, Jesse could see that Greg had splashed water on his face and looked a bit more awake.

"Find anything?" he asked Jesse.

"Nothing to write home about," said Jesse. "I did find an Ahren's Creek ..."

Greg brightened. "Really? Where?"

"Australia," Jesse reported glumly.

"Shit," said Greg.

"We're going to have a helluva time running down those four names. We need a date of birth or an area where they're from to narrow down the search at all. Facebook is littered with those names and it would take forever trying to run them down. It might be worthwhile posting their names on the various social media sites and see if we come up with something but even that would be a huge undertaking. I guess we're lucky they don't have more common names."

"What about the claim record?"

"So far, everything seems to lead back to the BLM as the keeper of the records. The BLM was established back in 1946 after the General Land Office, established in 1812, and the U.S. Grazing Service merged. I ran a search of location of the claim and the four claimants through the BLM's General Land Office records but got nothing. Someone who is more conversant on that site might do better. It's going to take some digging, though."

"In . . ." Jesse stopped to look at his watch, ". . . two and a half hours all I've done is scratch the surface. I reckon we need to find a real live researcher to help." He was expecting opposition from Greg and was surprised when none was forthcoming.

"I was afraid of that," said Greg, "I don't suppose you have anyone in mind?"

"Hardly. I'm afraid neither one of us is the researching

type."

"You'd be right about that. Where can we find such a person?"

"I just ran a search for a 'researcher' online and got a bunch of hits. Finding the right one will be the tough part. Maybe we should ask around the Intelligence Office. There are analysts there, maybe one of them knows someone, or is willing to take this on as a side job," Jesse suggested.

"Meanwhile," said Greg, "what'll we do with these papers and the nugget?"

"Let's make copies of the papers then put the originals and the nugget in a safe deposit box."

"Yeah, that's what I was thinking too. *And* we can't tell anyone anything about what we're doing. Agreed?"

Jesse nodded. "Monday I'll get a safe deposit box and, if you're up to it, we'll find out about a researcher. Now that I think about it, I know a guy in Intelligence, he's a photo interpreter. Maybe he'd know of someone."

"I don't think anything we're doing is illegal, do you?"

"Not yet but I did learn that if we go digging in land that's in a national monument or park, an Indian reservation, a military reservation, or a wildlife protection area we'll be in trouble. I don't think you can even file a claim on those lands."

"That figures. The federal government is pretty stingy," groused Greg.

"Yeah, they only let us search and dig on millions of acres. I just hope the mine isn't on the BMGR. That will complicate things," Jesse observed.

"I don't have any idea if I was on the bombing range or even the Cabeza Prieta Wildlife Refuge when I punched out," said Greg.

"And that's only where you found the saddlebags, God knows how far the claim is from there." He looked at his watch and said, "I'm *almost* late for a date with Susan. Hey, she works in personnel, maybe she knows of someone who can do our research."

"I don't see any reason not to ask her, just don't say too much, okay?"

"We should have some kind of cover story cooked up but that won't fly for long if we find someone who can help us."

"I guess we'll have to use our instincts on whom to trust. Matter of fact, what do your instincts tell you about Susan? You've been seeing her nearly four months, do you think she's trustworthy like we're looking for?"

"I would trust her with my life," said Jesse with confidence, "She wouldn't tell a soul."

"Well, kinda sound her out tonight and if your gut tells you she won't open her mouth, confide in her. But you know what they say, 'The security of a secret is directly proportional to how many people know about it,'" Greg admonished.

"I know and believe me, I'll be careful. Gotta go. I guess I just *assumed* you weren't up to going to dinner at the O (Officer's) Club. I don't think we'll be late. Want me to bring you back something?"

"Nah, I'm good. See you later."

CHAPTER 5

First Lieutenant Susan Liu was an assistant personnel officer at Davis-Monthan Air Force Base. She was petite, at five foot three, with short black hair, brown eyes and a pixyish upturn to her freckled nose. She was Eurasian, twenty-seven, never married, well-proportioned, and severely smitten with Jesse Grimes. She hadn't told him yet as she was as yet unsure of his feelings for her, but she was hopeful.

She walked into the O Club wearing a dark blue sleeveless cocktail dress that made eyes follow her from all over the club, but her eyes were searching only for the handsome pilot who had captured her heart. She was pleased that he was already sitting at a table and that he stood up when she approached to usher her into her chair. She didn't notice that Jesse had picked his table well, and it was out of hearing distance of other diners.

"Hi there," she whispered as he kissed her cheek and eased her chair up to their table.

"I'm glad you're late – well, later than me – I wasn't sure I was going to make it on time. Did you hear about Greg Miller?"

"No! What happened?" she asked as the waiter handed her a menu.

"Go ahead and order a drink first if you want one," Jesse suggested.

She ordered a vodka tonic and after the waiter turned to leave, she looked askance at her date.

"Greg had a malfunction in his aircraft during a training mission yesterday and had to punch out. He was in the hospital with a broken kneecap. They did surgery on him to repair the kneecap and he was released this afternoon.. He should recover a hundred percent and come back to flight status."

"Oh no! Where did this happen?"

"He was coming off a strafing run on the BMGR and lost power over the Growler Mountains west of Ajo. His plane crashed north of Growler Peak, but, like I said, he'll be alright."

"Is there anything I can do?" she asked.

"Maybe indirectly," Jesse said vaguely.

"Indirectly? So I shouldn't plan on cleaning his bedroom or baking him a pie?" she asked mischievously.

"Right," said Jesse then looked around them almost furtively. "What I'm going to tell you has to stay between you, me and Greg; it's imperative that the word not get out." Curiosity piqued, Susan nodded for Jesse to continue. "I wouldn't trust this with anyone but you."

Jesse, you'll never know how safe your secret is with me!

"After he ejected and landed, Greg crawled into a cave to spend the night and discovered a pair of old saddlebags buried in the dirt. There were some papers, and a gold nugget in a pouch The letter was dated 1889 from one prospector to one of his partners and reported that two other partners had been killed by Indians and the partner writing the letter was in a bad way. It spoke of a gold claim *somewhere* – we have no idea where – and there was a receipt for forty-two ounces of gold and a copy of a mining claim application.

"The description of the location of the mine was vague at best and all of our computer checks today got us nowhere. We finally decided we needed to find a professional – or at least an avid and experienced amateur – researcher to help us learn as much as we can about the prospectors, where the mine is and the status of the gold left in the Yuma Bank and Trust, if such an entity still exists.

"We thought that *maybe*, being a personnel officer, you might have suggestions about finding a competent, trustworthy researcher. Advertising in the paper or online are not attractive options because we don't know what kind of person we'd be getting and we think this needs to stay quiet.

"So there you have it, the big secret. Oh, the nugget in the pouch weighed about two ounces and was assayed at eighty-seven percent pure. We checked the current price of gold and it's around $1800 an ounce for pure gold."

"That's a lot to take in, Jesse," said Susan, almost at a loss for words. But she exulted that Jesse trusted her enough to confide in her! "That's quite a project to take on considering the mining equipment you'd need ..."

"Oh, I almost forgot. This is a placer gold claim, not a hard rock operation so there won't be a need for drilling equipment, and dynamite and all that. In broad strokes, you pull out the gravel and sediment in a river or creek bed, screen out the big stuff and pan the gold out of what's left."

"That sounds a little more manageable for two Air Force pilots in their spare time who don't know the first thing about mining," said Susan. "Would it be a good idea to find a knowledgeable prospector and work with him for a while? I can't think of a better way to learn the trade than by doing it under the supervision of someone with experience. That would also be a good way to learn firsthand what equipment you're going to need.

"I would think that finding researchers would be easy, finding a *good* one who is scrupulously honest will be the challenge. Did you look online for researchers?"

"Yep. I found a ton, but again it boils down to trust and pickin' one out of the yellow pages just don't feel right," Jesse replied.

Susan nodded. "There are all kinds of professional researchers, from genealogical to scientific. Even private investigators can save you untold hours just because they have subscriptions to various information sources. And price is an issue. How much can you pay him or her, or are you going to go on a contingency basis and pay only if the search is successful?"

"I'm pretty well connected in personnel circles and have

encountered dozens of investigators who, by another name, are sometimes researchers. Let me look through my contacts, maybe someone will jump out at me. Meanwhile, let's order dinner."

"I was kind of hoping you might have a close friend that you could recommend."

Susan paused as if in thought. "Hmm, I just might. I assume you prefer someone located in Arizona in order to defray expenses?"

Jesse nodded then picked up his menu. "Thank you for listening, Susan, and taking this seriously."

She smiled. "The story is too fantastic to be a hoax. I think I know someone, but we'd better run it by Greg first. Why don't we go see him after dinner?" She steered the conversation away from the gold claim, "What did you do when Greg crashed?"

"I was halfway back to Tucson when he called in his mayday. I turned around and went back to search for him in case he managed to get out of the plane. It was like I was almost flying blind in the dark trying to see if he managed to eject. I was flying way lower than I was supposed to, hoping to see a light or hear him broadcast with his portable radio. I was feeling pretty low by the time I had to return to base. Turns out he broke his portable emergency radio when he landed and his locator beacon didn't activate.""

"That must have been a terrible feeling."

"The worst. He's my best friend and we've been flying together for a long time, including two deployments to the Middle East." Jesse stared off into space for a moment until she brought him back to the present.

"Well, he's home and he's safe so quit dwelling on what might have been." Jesse smiled and nodded.

They discussed going out to the Sonora Desert Museum over the coming weekend. Susan had been there before and was eager to show Jesse the wonderful exhibits on display since he had never been there. They finished dinner and walked hand in hand out to Jesse's SUV where he opened Susan's door for her. Before climbing into the 4x4, she turned, put her arms around his waist and drew him to her. "You're a good friend," she whispered and kissed him.

It took about twenty minutes to drive to Greg and Jesse's apartment on Houghton Road. They found Greg lying on the couch with a pillow under his knee. He was finishing a baloney and cheese sandwich and watching cartoons – the Roadrunner.

"I see you're improving your mind while nourishing your body," Jesse cracked.

"Well, I had to do something. No one around here cares enough to wait on me so I had to fend for myself," Greg retorted righteously.

"I'm just pleased to see that your fending for yourself didn't include getting pie-eyed. That doesn't mix well with painkillers," said Susan.

"What are you two doing here anyway?" Greg asked.

"We were talking about your 'problem' and Susan thought she might have a solution," said Jesse. He looked over at her.

"I happen to have a lifelong friend who works at the Pima County Library. We went to high school and college together in New Hampshire, and a year ago she followed me to Tucson. She's a keen genealogical investigator and what she can't find at work, she usually uncovers through information subscriptions at home. I don't think she's ever taken on a case quite like this but she thrives on tracking down historical people and places."

"She sounds almost too good to be true," observed Greg.

"I know what you mean," said Susan. "Can she keep her mouth shut? All I can tell you is that she's from New England where people are typically close-mouthed and once, in high school, she wouldn't even tell me my boyfriend was going out with another girl. When I asked her about it, she said she thought it was none of her business and it wasn't her place to butt in. I wasn't too pleased with her at the time, but grew to respect her regard for other people's privacy. I'd trust her with my life and those of my children if I had any."

"I don't reckon you'd make such a recommendation lightly," said Jesse. He looked at his watch, then said, "It's only six o'clock on a Tuesday, y'all think she might come over for a chat this evening?"

"Well, I know she isn't seeing anyone right now. I guess I could call her . . ."

"That would be great, Susan. Do you agree, Jesse?" asked Greg enthusiastically. Jesse nodded. In a way they had nothing to lose unless they spilled their secret with a blabbermouth, and, from what he knew of this girl, she wasn't one. "Yep. If you think it's a good idea, Susan, go ahead on."

Susan nodded and pulled her cell phone from her purse. She punched in a number and the men could hear it ring once, then twice. They heard someone say "Hello," then Susan asked, "What are you doing?"

They couldn't hear the rest of the other side of the conversation but Susan explained the nature of the call without divulging the classified part, and invited her friend to come to the apartment "for a meeting."

"Great," said Susan, "I'll see you in about half an hour." She hung up and smiled. "She's on the way."

CHAPTER 6

Jenevive Belle Isle, Jen to her friends, was twenty-seven and had never married. She was five feet six inches tall, slender with dark, shoulder-length hair and a fair complexion that belied her French-Canadian ancestry. She laughed easily, but was ferociously loyal to her few friends and her Yankee heritage. She had earned a double degree from Dartmouth in Library and Computer Sciences and few people knew that she was a closet computer hacker. She didn't hack often or for profit but sometimes bureaucratic red tape pissed her off and she found a way around it.

She parked in the lot in Greg and Jesse's complex and approached the ground floor apartment. *This had better not be a left-hand attempt at a blind date.* Susan had done that to her before, and her guard was up. Jesse, whom she knew fairly well, answered the door.

"Hi Jen," Jesse said with a smile and opening the door wide, "come on in, the party is just starting."

"Party? I thought this was supposed to be . . .,"

"Just a figure of speech, Jen," Jesse interrupted, "we're here to talk, not to dance and raise hell – no booze, unless you want a glass of wine."

Relieved, Jen walked past Jesse into the living room. She saw Susan sitting on a love seat and a friend of Jesse's, she thought, stretched out on the couch. His right knee was elevated and surrounded by a black knee brace. She had seen him before, once or twice, and thought his name was Greg.

"Hey!" said Greg.

"Hi," said Jen, still a little bit on her guard.

"Have a seat," said Susan, nodding toward an easy chair

opposite the couch. "You know Greg, right? Greg Miller, Jen Belle Isle."

Greg nodded then said, "Please forgive me for not getting up, I kind of messed up my knee the other day and standing is tough."

Jen waved off the apology then looked pointedly at her friend of many years. In turn, Susan looked at first Jesse, then at Greg as if getting permission to proceed. When both nodded, she began, "A unique situation has presented itself that requires a skill set like yours. The guys are very concerned about keeping the matter confidential. If we tell you about it and you choose not to become involved, they'll need your promise that it won't go any further than this room. I know you well enough to know it won't if you say it won't, but they don't know you as well as I do."

"As long as it's nothing illegal, I promise," said Jen, looking first at Jesse then at Greg.

Silence filled the room for thirty seconds until Greg sighed audibly, then told his story. When he finished, Jen said, "Sounds like you could use someone who knows where and how to research the information you're looking for. You probably won't find much, if anything, doing routine internet searches ..."

"I reckon we already found that out," said Jesse ruefully.

Jen glanced at him as she continued, "... like Google. You will probably need to go to various facilities and hand search records because most government agencies can't afford to go back and computerize their early early records. I assume you're trying to confirm the deaths of the prospectors since locating birth certificates really only tells you who their ancestors were. Death certificates don't tell you much either, unless you're lucky enough to find an obituary which has relatives, previous residences and so on. Even that won't help you a great deal.

Court and government records are where you'll find what you need including records of the claim and improvements done to it plus current ownership if there is a current owner. Government surveys, maps and plats are where you might find a lead on Ahren's

41

Seep. That will be the hardest one to locate and, of course, the one most valuable to you. This will require hand searches in the Yuma County and probably Pima County Archives, and that is labor intensive. It becomes a matter of how much you want to spend unless you get very lucky early on. You already know when the claim was filed and that will help a lot but those files might now belong to BLM, or one of the other federal agencies."

"That brings up the question of cost," said Jesse. "What do you charge?"

"I charge twenty-five dollars an hour whether I'm on a computer or thumbing through papers, microfiche or microfilm," she replied.

"That's almost what my base pay is!" Jesse exclaimed.

Jen smiled. "I don't get the fringe package you do, which is usually worth another $25,000 a year."

"You got me there," Jesse admitted then thought for a minute. "Do you ever work on a contingency basis?" he asked, as if the idea had just occurred to him.

"I've been asked that before, usually by attorneys, and my answer has always been no. But then, I'm not real fond of how attorneys conduct their business for the most part."

"What about in our case?" Jesse pressed.

"What are you offering?" Jen countered.

Jesse looked at Greg and raised his eyebrows.

Greg looked at Susan who raised her arms chest high with her palms facing outward and shook her head.

He looked back at his wing man then blurted, "Ten percent?"

It was Jen's turn to look pensive. Then a thought struck her, "Including ten percent of the value of the nugget? That way at least I'll get expenses out of this if it turns out to be a dry hole."

It was Greg's turn to raise his eyebrows to Jesse, who immediately nodded.

Greg paused, then said, "Ten percent including ten percent of the value of the nugget."

"Done," said Jen. She rose and walked over to Greg, reached down, and shook his hand, then Jesse's and, finally, Susan's. "Any chance I can get the ten percent of the nugget up front? I'm going to be burning up a lot of gas between here and Yuma."

"Will you take a check?" asked Greg.

"Sure."

"Then we have a deal. When can you start and what can we do to help? Apparently, I'm immobile for the next few weeks but I can work on my laptop if that will help."

"Your timing is perfect. I'm on furlough from the library due to the Co-Vid 19 virus, I can start right away. I'll give you the passwords to my online information sources and you can be checking them for the prospectors while I'm in Yuma looking for information on the claim and Ahren's Seep."

"What about us?" asked Susan.

"I suggest you find someone who will buy gold, like the nugget - not necessarily to sell it, but to learn what you can about the buying and selling of gold. That will be necessary especially if we find the claim and put some gold on the market. The gold market is rife with crooks so keep your guard up."

"What about tracing back the National Yuma Bank and Trust to see if they have the original gold deposited, and if they don't, who does?" asked Greg.

"It seems to me," said Jen, "that an account can be declared dormant after three to five years at which time the property is surrendered to the state. The owner has, if I'm not mistaken, another three years to file a claim. If no claim is filed, the property is sold at auction by the state. The process is called escheatmet."

"So, after over a hundred and thirty years, the gold left in the Yuma Bank and Trust is long gone," observed Greg.

"I might be wrong and someone should double check me, but I think that's the situation."

"There goes about $80,000 we could have used for start up costs," said Jesse with a snort.

"It's still worth checking but don't get your hopes up."

"Susan and I can do that since it might require some leg work," said Jesse. "My darling girlfriend also suggested one of us hire on with an experienced prospector for a while to learn something about the process. *Some* people will do anything to get out of a little hard work, including destroying an eighteen-million-dollar aircraft belonging to Uncle Sam, so I guess that someone will be me."

Greg grinned. "I'll have you know I did so at great personal risk."

"I'm sure you did," said Susan with a smirk, then brought the meeting back on track. "Is there anything else we ought to be doing?"

"One thing I always do when I open a new case is to set up an accounts receivable/accounts payable ledger. Take it from me, it's almost impossible to remember all your expenses at the end of a week much less a month. Of course, usually accounts payable is much more memorable but it's still a good idea to keep track as you go along."

Everyone looked at Greg. He grimaced in resignation then said, "Oh sure. One term of accounting and I get stuck. Crap!"

"Well, if that's everything," Susan began, "I think we should celebrate with a glass of wine – except for Greg, of course."

"Thanks a lot," grumbled Greg. But the smile that followed made it clear that he was in agreement.

Susan got up and went into the kitchen. She returned minutes later with an open bottle of wine and three glasses. She set them on the coffee table then returned for a glass of orange juice for the invalid.

"Thanks, Susan," said Greg, "as soon as you pour the wine I'll propose a toast." Soon everyone was raising a glass to the Cactus Wren Claim.

"So, Jen," said Susan, "why don't you tell the guys a little about yourself. They already know you're from New Hampshire."

"That's all you told them?" Jen asked incredulously, "Usually you tell everyone my whole life story and they wind up telling me things about myself I'm not sure I knew."

"Let's see, New Hampshire. You went to Dartmouth, right?" asked Jesse. She nodded and he continued, "I've heard about their rowdy Homecomings. Sounds like quite a tradition."

"It is." she agreed. "I used to go back every year but the farther I get from home the less likely it is that I'll return."

"The University of Arizona has a similar tradition but the school isn't nearly as old as Dartmouth; it was only established in 1885," Greg offered. "I've taken some classes there and it seems like a good enough school but I haven't participated in any extracurricular activities. Of course it's just past, but the Tucson Festival of Books is a great function if you're into books. The University of Arizona is one of the sponsors. I attended the past two years and got to meet some very interesting people including several well-known authors."

"I liked the festival too," Jen exclaimed. "I guess we could have walked right by each other and not known it. I got to meet three of my favorite authors which was pretty exciting."

"Who did you meet?" asked Greg, genuinely interested.

"Let's see, there was Cindy McGhee. She wrote *New York Burning, Power House* and *Evil Tides.*"

"I read *New York Burning,*" said Greg, "I really liked it."

Jen nodded. "Then I met Ian Michaels, who wrote *Lantern Light* and *Opening Gambit.*" Greg shook his head. "And then I got to meet Donna Truxton. She wrote . . ."

"*Roadrunner Freedom, Keep a Small Fire* and *The Mesa Has Ears.* I read them all," Greg interrupted. "I like to read stuff that is located in the area in which I live."

"Yeah! Me too. I especially liked *Keep a Small Fire.*" Greg nodded enthusiastically then realized that Jesse and Susan weren't talking. He looked over at them and blushed red, they were both smirking at him.

"What? Don't you two ever *read* anything."

"Of course, we were just trying to get a word in edgewise," said Susan smugly. Secretly she had had hopes that something might kindle between these two and now, maybe it had.

Greg looked over at Jen and rolled his eyes then whispered, "I know for a fact that Jesse can barely write his name without misspelling it. I don't know how he got into the Air Force, much less became a pilot."

Jesse just stuck his nose in the air and looked away. "I'll not dignify that with a response," he said haughtily.

"If it wasn't for Greg's knee, next thing you know they'd be rolling around on the floor muttering;

"I can too spell."

"Can not."

"Can too."

"Before any blood is spilled," asked Jen, "can I have a copy of your documents for reference?"

"Sure," said Greg, "Jesse, can you run them off for her?"

Jesse did so without comment and Jen stuffed them into her hand bag. "I think I'm going to head home and get to work. Um, who should I call when or if I find something?" she asked.

"Oh, wait," said Greg, "I need to write you a check."

"Why don't we use Greg as a clearing house for the next few weeks? At least he should be near his phone most of the time. You can get the number off his check," suggested Susan with a sly grin.

CHAPTER 7

Less than fifteen minutes after Jen left, Greg's phone rang.

"This is Greg," he answered.

"Hi, it's me," said Jen, hoping he would recognize her voice.

"Hey. Jeez, I haven't talked to you in a good ten minutes!" he joked.

"About this project, I just wanted to reassure you that I will keep this confidential, you don't have to worry."

"I never doubted it for a minute. Are you home already?"

"No, I'm at a red light down on Broadway and . . .OH MY GOD!"

The sound of crashing drowned out Jen's voice then there was silence.

"Jen? Jen, are you there?" asked Greg, highly agitated.

"What?" said Jesse and Susan at once. "What's wrong?" Susan demanded.

"It's Jen," Greg explained, "I think she's been involved in an accident. C'mon, let's go, she's somewhere down on Broadway."

"You can't go," protested Susan, "you're a wreck already."

"Like hell I can't," Greg gritted his teeth as he struggled to his foot and grabbed his crutches. "She told me she was stopped at a red light on Broadway. C'mon, it can't be that far."

They rushed out to Jesse's Highlander and he backed out of the parking space and tore down Houghton to Broadway. He turned left on Broadway and sped down the four-lane highway, looking for Jen's Honda. Jesse blew red lights at Kolb and Craycroft, before pulling up behind her Honda at Alvernon. There were no other cars around or police cars, and they could see that Jen was still in the car.

Susan was the first to arrive at Jen's driver's door. Jen was looking down and crying.

Susan tapped on Jen's window and Jen jumped then turned and, seeing her friend, opened the door. As she got out of the car, Susan could see that the young woman had small pieces of glass in her hair and all over the front of her. Jen also had several very minor cuts on her right arm and face.

By the time Jen emerged from the car, Greg and Jesse had made their way over to the girls' location. Susan had begun to brush glass off her friend.

"Jen?" asked Greg, "what happened?"

"There was this guy," she began through her sobs. "I was stopped at the light talking to Greg when the guy ran up to the side of my car, and the window exploded. He grabbed my purse and was gone." Then she began to wail, "The mine papers! They were in my purse!"

"Jen? Can you describe the man at all?"

"No, all I saw was a hoodie over his head, and something in his hand that shattered the window and then he was gone. It happened so fast!"

"I'll call Tucson PD," said Greg.

"What good will that do, she didn't see the guy," asked Susan.

"Her insurance company will want a police report number and I have to believe that the district cops around here would like to know there's a smash and grab robber operating in the area."

"Jen?" asked Greg, "are you okay to wait here to talk to the police?"

Jen nodded. She had stopped sobbing and was blowing her nose with a tissue provided by her friend. Greg walked up to her and grasped her gently by both arms.

"Don't worry about the mine papers. The thief will take your money, maybe your credit cards and dump the purse. I wouldn't be surprised if the police recover it in a day or two. You okay? Do you need to see a doctor?" he asked, noting the tiny cuts on her face and arm.

Greg then enfolded Jen in his arms and just held her, flabbergasting Susan,. He could feel her relax against him and knew it was the right thing to do.

Four minutes later a Tucson Police Department patrol car with its overheads flashing pulled up behind Jesse's SUV. A young Hispanic woman, in uniform, emerged from the car and approached. "I'm Officer Diaz, what's going on?" she asked.

The trio of friends let Jen make her own report without interrupting. When she finished, Officer Diaz said, "This is the third report I've taken tonight – woman by herself in the car, stopped at a light, and wham, the bad guy shatters the window, grabs what he can and runs. Almost impossible to prevent and to apprehend the guy unless he tries to use the credit cards somewhere at a later time."

"The best thing we can do is get your driver's license and all your credit cards into the computer as fast as possible and hope the bad guy tries to use them."

"I'll call in the numbers as soon as I get home," said Jen.

Officer Diaz nodded. After shooting some pictures of the car and Jen's face, she gave Jen a report number, walked back to her patrol car and drove away.

"Well, there's no sense in standing around out here," said Greg. "Jen, are you up to driving home with Susan or would you like Jesse and me to run you home and Susan can follow in your car? I thought if you girls drove home, Jesse and I could drive around the area a little and maybe spot your purse."

The girls talked softly between themselves, then Susan announced that they would leave in Jen's car and go to Susan's apartment and wait for the men there. Jen was understandably skittish about going back home when the bad guy now knew where she lived from her driver's license in her purse.

Greg and Jesse got back in the SUV and began a slow creep of the neighborhood but their search proved fruitless.

They arrived at Susan's apartment complex in time to see the girls trying to tape plastic into the broken window space. Jen had settled down from the attack and wasn't nearly as shaky as she had been when they first found her.

"Thanks for looking, you guys. I've been dreading the thought of having to go get another driver's license and all that other stuff."

"I doubt the thief even noted your address but it wouldn't hurt to be a little extra vigilant," said Greg.

Jen handed him a business card with all her information on it and, as an afterthought, gave one to Jesse, *just in case.* Susan would know where Jen was most of the time but if Jesse had information for her, it was best to be connected to everyone.

"I'd invite everyone in for a drink but I don't have anything except some very old ouzo which I doubt anyone would like. It was left over from a party months ago and . . . I just haven't thrown it out yet".

They all said their goodbyes and went their separate ways. Greg found himself thinking about Jen and worrying if she was okay.

*****

Officer Veronica Diaz was pissed. Three times! Three times in one shift some mope in her district had robbed lone women in their cars! It was embarrassing and frustrating because she knew the odds of catching the bastard were nil, especially since her shift ended in twenty minutes. She thought about going to her Watch Commander and getting him to organize an after-shift-task force to go after the SOB but she knew he would never authorize the overtime.

In seven and a half years she had never had anything like this happen. The perp was like a boil on her butt that wouldn't go away! Veronica lived in one of the new apartments on Old Spanish Trail and decided she'd take Broadway back across town on her way home. She would be alone in her own car and if she happened to stop for a stop light on the way and the perp showed, he wouldn't get away for the fourth time. If he missed her the first time through, maybe she would make a second trip through just in case.

Veronica returned to the PD at her usual time and changed into her street clothes. She was getting pumped. She got in her car and placed her off-duty 9mm Smith and Wesson automatic on the passenger seat under a towel – within easy reach. *Let the bastard come!*

Veronica eased out of the parking lot and made her way over to Broadway and headed east. *Showtime.* There were two cars near her going the same way when Veronica turned onto Broadway but they turned off before she had gone a quarter of a mile. *Perfect.* She slowed to just under the speed limit and made sure to stay in the outside lane. Every time she stopped for a red light, her right hand crept under the towel. Finally, as she slowed for a light somewhere between Kolb and Pantano, she caught a glimpse of a shadow of a person running toward the right rear quarter of her car. As the car stopped, Veronica reached for the 9mm just as the shadow reached her passenger window and, even though she was prepared for it, she was shocked by the violence as the window shattered. She didn't have time to say anything before she raised the 9mm and fired twice point blank at the perpetrator. The person staggered back away from the car and made it to the sidewalk before he collapsed.

Veronica shifted her car into Park and, still holding the 9mm, jumped from the car and ran to where the perpetrator had collapsed on his right side on the concrete. She could see he was still breathing and was bleeding from a shoulder wound but the blood was not pumping out as it would have had she hit an artery. She pulled her spare handcuffs out of her jacket pocket and ratcheted them onto the perp's wrists then retrieved her phone and dialed 911. She identified herself and reported that shots had been fired and there was a man down and gave the location. She unzipped his hoodie and found herself looking at a teenaged Hispanic male with only one wound, just above his left collarbone. She took his do-rag off and jammed it against the wound to stop the trickle of blood.

"You shot me," he moaned."

"It happens when you rob people."

"I didn't have no gun," he whined.

"You had something dangerous enough to shatter my window. Flying glass could have blinded me."

"Listen to me," Veronica told the young man, "I'm a police officer and you are under arrest. You need to listen while I advise you of your rights." She rattled off the perp's Constitutional rights admonishment then asked, are you willing to make a statement?"

"I don't feel so good."

"The ambulance is on its way. Who were you working with?"

"It was just me."

"But you were taking the proceeds of the robberies to someone."

"Alfredo," the perp groaned. "I need a doctor."

"One's on the way, just try to relax. What's Alfredo's last name?"

"Menendez."

"Where does he live?"

"Over in South Tucson, I forget the address but it's on Camino Verde."

"How did you get over here from South Tucson?"

"Alfredo drove. He parked a couple of blocks away when I did the job."

"What kind of car was Alfredo driving?"

"I think it's a Chevy."

"What model?"

"I don't know. It's a big car."

"What color is it?"

Veronica could hear sirens approaching. She retrieved her

off duty badge from a jacket pocket and draped it around her neck on a chain in preparation for identifying herself.

"What color is Alfredo's car?"

"Green and white."

The rescue truck was the first to arrive. The two paramedics ran over with their equipment trunks. One of them nudged Veronica back and said, "We'll take over from here. Hey partner, how you doing?" the paramedic asked as he lifted the do-rag off the wound.

"She shot me," he said, pointing at Veronica accusingly.

"Someone sure did," said the paramedic, "do you hurt anywhere else?"

"No, but I'm in a lot of pain, can you give me a shot or something?"

"Pretty soon. I need to check you over first. What's your name?"

"Paco, Paco Gutierrez."

Veronica was still close enough to hear the exchange. "Paco," she asked, "where were you taking the stuff you were got from the women you robbed?"

"I gave it all to Alfredo. I was only getting part of the cash."

"What was Alfredo going to do with the other stuff?"

"I don't know. He takes it home then tries to sell it."

"So you two have done this before?"

There was a long silence as the paramedic worked. Then Paco said, "I don't think I want to talk to you anymore. I don't want to get Alfredo in no trouble.

"That's your right but covering for Alfredo seems like a losing proposition. I mean, he's making you do all the dangerous stuff and he's getting part of the cash and all the other stuff. I don't see him here trying to help you."

Paco remained silent. "How is he?" Veronica asked.

"He'll be fine, it looks like the bullet went all the way through and through the muscle and didn't lodge in the shoulder. There's some cloth fragments in there from his shirt but nothing that can't be cleaned out. That's not to say he's going to be pain free in a day or two."

Two police cars arrived simultaneously, one of them the Watch Commander. They maneuvered Officer Diaz away from the others and Lieutenant Richardson asked her if she was okay.

She nodded in the affirmative but she could feel herself starting to get a little shaky from the adrenaline spike. "You look like it's time to sit down," said the Lieutenant as he gently escorted her over to his car and sat her down in the front seat.

"Where's your weapon?" he asked.

"In its holster under the front driver's seat." The Lieutenant directed one of the arriving patrolmen to secure it. She was glad she took the time to secure the weapon; had it still been on the front seat of the car under the towel, it might not have looked too good.

"So what happened?" asked the Watch Commander.
Veronica went through the whole story truthfully though she tried to shade it to look like she was just going home but taking precautions because of what had occurred on her shift. She included her rights admonishment to Paco Gutierrez and the statements he made to her. The Lieutenant called over a sergeant and directed him to call out a couple of robbery detectives. The Lieutenant, a former detective himself, recognized the makings of a search warrant when he heard them.

"We're going to treat this like it is, an officer-involved-shooting and one of the standard procedures is to replace your weapon with another so we can run tests on yours. You're not under suspicion of anything and it's all standard procedure. A shooting team will be called out and will conduct the investigation. While that's going on, after you're interviewed, we'll need you to write a report on what transpired here. You already turned in the other three robbery reports?"

Veronica nodded. "If the detectives get a search warrant for Alfredo's car and house, can I go?"

"I doubt it, but I'll ask. It might look too much like a conflict of interest. We'll let the detectives earn their money. Besides, it looks like some pieces of flying glass nicked your face and we ought to have the paramedics look at them while they're here."

Disappointed, Veronica only nodded. *At least I put a stop to it.* She thought of calling the victims but decided that was the detectives' place. She'd have to be satisfied with her part being unsung. After all, it wasn't like she was looking for glory, just a little credit for a job well done.

Once Paco Gutierrez was loaded in the ambulance and driven away, one of the paramedics led Veronica over to a first aid truck. He daubed the several nicks with antiseptic but didn't bandage them since they were so small. A forensic photographer walked over and took several pictures of her cuts then one of the lead detectives sat her in the front seat of his car so he could interview her. He taped her interview, which she knew was SOP, but it made her edgy nevertheless. She had taped plenty of suspects in the very same way. Once the detective had finished the interview, he turned Veronica over to the Watch Commander who sent her home with instructions to write her report on her department-issued laptop then email it back to the department. Once she was turned loose, she sought out the lead investigator and asked him to let her know how the search warrant turned out. He agreed that he would. Finally, she went home. She wondered if she would feel the usual after effects from shooting another human being but so far, she just felt tired as she wrote her report as directed.

It was four thirty in the morning and she debated having a drink, then decided against it and went to bed instead.

CHAPTER 8

Getting a search warrant for a person, place or thing isn't a twenty-minute proposition like it is on TV and in the movies. It takes hours just to write the damned affidavit. It has to be approved by a prosecutor then, if it's the middle of the night, you have to wake up a judge which can make for a dicey situation since most judges are prima donnas and don't *like* their sleep disturbed. Grumpy, they'll grudgingly take time to read through the affidavit and exhibits before usually deciding there is probable cause to search the person, place or thing and sign the warrant.

So it was for Alfredo, his vehicle and his home. Next a search team had to be gathered and a raid plan devised so everyone on the raid knew their job. After all, you are often forcing an entry into a person's home which is always dangerous.

They were taking no chances with Alfredo Menendez's search warrant. The raid team found the green and white Chevrolet Caprice parked in front of a small, cinder block home with the right address on it. A reasonable length of time was given between the knock and announce and the crash of the "key" (a heavy one-person battering ram) as it forced open the door. After ensuring there were no weapons secreted in the couch in the living room, all persons in the house, i.e. Alfredo, his wife and children, were handcuffed and searched – well, the adults were - then led into the living room and seated on the couch while the rest of the house was secured. They were advised of their rights and both declined to make a statement after the search warrant was read to them.

A thorough search of the premises and vehicle ensued, and certain items were found including cash, three purses that clearly didn't belong to Mrs. Menendez, their contents and the three documents stolen from Jen's purse. It was all seized as evidence and when the search was over it was transported to Tucson PD for processing.

It was late morning when her phone rang, Veronica Diaz had just fallen asleep and woke up disoriented. "Hello?" she mumbled groggily.

"Is this Officer Diaz?" asked a male voice.

"Uh huh," she said.

"Sorry to wake you up but you asked me to call when we finished the search warrant at Alfredo Menendez's house."

"Oh! Yes! How did it go? You're just getting done?" she asked, now wide awake.

"We got proceeds from all three of your robberies plus, I think, stuff from some previous smash and grabs. Mr. and Mr. Menendez clammed up immediately but based on what we found, and little Paco's statement to you, they're toast. Would you like to notify your victims from last night? Just let them know they should expect a grand jury subpoena within the next week or so. We'll also be calling them to arrange a release of the stuff they need back."

"Sure, I'll be glad to do that, I have their phone numbers here in my notebook. Thank you for calling."

"No problem. You did a good job out there, and it's the least we can do. Now get some sleep!" With that, the line went dead.

That the detectives hadn't raided a dry hole was a relief to Veronica, and she was happy to make the notifications to inform her victims that their property had been recovered and both suspects arrested, one after being shot. About an hour later, she finished talking with her very appreciative victims and tumbled back into bed.

Jen was so excited when she hung up the phone after talking with Officer Diaz she just had to tell someone. Susan's phone went to voice mail so she called Greg.

"Hello?" answered Greg.

"They caught 'em!" Jen exclaimed. "The police caught the

people who robbed me and shot one of them! They recovered all my stuff!"

"That's great news, Jen," said Greg with enthusiasm. "You get your stuff back and, if we're lucky, our secret stays safe. How're you feeling today?"

"After news like that, I'm more than fine." she replied, "I was just getting ready to start calling people to cancel credit cards and stuff."

"Good. Now get back to work!" Greg said and laughed.

"Yes sir. As soon as I get my license back, I'm headed for Yuma," she said with chuckle. "I'm eager to start researching the claim and Ahren's Seep. Surely there has to be mention of it somewhere in the courthouse records. You probably have the best feel for the geography involved, got any good guesses?"

"Boy, I've given that a lot of thought! I figure, roughly, that it's a hundred miles from Yuma to Ajo, as the buzzard flies. I'm just guessing that the mine is closer to Ajo than Yuma only because of where I found the saddlebags and, as the county boundaries are now, where the claim is, is likely in Pima County. Did those early records get transferred to Pima County from Yuma County when the boundary was established? I don't know but my uneducated guess says no so I think you're right to be searching in Yuma County even though my best guess is that the claim is now in Pima County and probably within Cabeza Prieta Wildlife Refuge boundaries which is off-limits for prospecting. I hope I'm wrong, and the mine is on BLM land but my experience has been that Murphy and his Law love me."

"Do you have a good topographical map of the area you're talking about?"

Greg chuckled. "Probably the best in the world but they frown on us using Air Force tactical maps for personal reasons," he said. "I would think a BLM map or a USGS (US Geological Survey) map would suffice but I don't have one."

"I thought, if we had a good map, you could show me the

area you're talking about and I could take it with me and work from it. I would think I could find something like that at the University of Arizona, wouldn't you?"

"Yes and I think having a few good maps will be the cornerstone of this search. I don't mean to sound indelicate but do you have the wherewithal to acquire them?"

She laughed. "I'll just take it out of my 'advance' unless you have a better idea."

Greg chuckled again. "That works for me if it works for you."

"I thought I'd acquire what we need, then come over so you can show me where you're talking about on the map. For all we know, Ahren's Seep is already marked."

Greg felt a little spike of adrenalin shoot through him at her suggestion. He didn't know why, after all, he didn't feel an attraction to her . . . he didn't think . . ." "Yeah, sure," he said "I'll definitely be here all day; I don't have a doctor's appointment until a week from Monday, unless there's a problem."

"Okay. I'll stop by the University and then I'll be over. Want me to bring lunch?"

"That would be terrific, I'll even reimburse you. Jesse didn't leave me too well supplied for today. He's going to the store on his way home tonight so I should be better off tomorrow – probably hot dogs."

"Anything you don't like?" she asked.

"Nah, I'm pretty easy."

They ended the conversation and Greg felt that same little surge of adrenaline. What the hell was going on and why did he feel the need to clean up a bit? After taking a sponge bath, shaving and brushing his teeth, Greg set to work with the public information sources whose access passwords were given to him by Jen. It didn't take him long to find death certificates for Albert Neal, Josiah Carter and Micah Clapton. After all, the Army had found and buried them and reported their deaths. Greg never found a trace of Jake

Humbertson. He had probably been killed by renegade Indians and left for the coyotes and vultures. His body was probably never found.

Inasmuch as Jesse was going to pick up an accounting ledger based on Jen's recommendation, Greg didn't have anything left on his list to do. He decided to look for Yuma Bank and Trust on Jen's websites. That was actually on Jesse and Susan's to do list, but both were working and Greg was sitting at home twiddling his thumbs.

It became clear rather quickly that the Yuma Bank and Trust was no longer in business since entries on the web were few. After a substantial amount of digging, he learned that the bank had merged three times with other financial institutions and was now part of 1st Bank Yuma. He called the bank and asked about records dating back to the late 1800s and was told that such records had probably been destroyed long ago but the clerk would check and call him back. *Like that's gonna happen.*

Just then his phone rang, "Hello?"

"Greg? It's Jen."

"Hey," said Greg, that little tickle was back.

"I thought I'd give you a heads up I'm almost there, so you have time to get up and open the door."

"No problem. I had Jesse leave the door unlocked when he left for work this morning."

"Okay. See you in a few." Five minutes later there was a tap at Greg's door and it opened.

"Just me," said Jen, "don't shoot; I have lunch."

"Well then, c'mon in," said Greg. He was seated lengthwise on the couch, with his back propped up against the armrest with a pillow. His right leg was straight out and there was a pillow behind his right knee. "Welcome to the sick, lame and lazy department," he said with a rueful grin.

"Hope you're hungry. I almost bought out the deli hoping to find something you'd like." She had two large plastic bags in her hand as she half turned to close the door. One was labeled

"University of Arizona," and the other bore the logo for "Solomon's Deli."

"Like I said, I'm easy, I'll eat most anything. Whatever is left over I can have for lunch tomorrow."

Jen laid the U of A bag down on the couch at Greg's feet. The other she placed on the coffee table and started pulling out wrapped parcels whose smells made Greg's mouth water.

"Let's see, this one is a Reuben . . . this one is roast beef with cheddar . . . and here's a turkey and cranberry. Anything sound good yet?"

"I'd go for the Reuben, unless you want it," said Greg, eyeing the food.

"Perfect. I'll take the turkey and cranberry. There's also potato chips, potato salad and coleslaw."

"You pick," said Greg.

"I think I'd rather have the coleslaw unless you want it."

"The potato salad is fine with me."

Finally she pulled out two bottles of infused water and set them on the coffee table. "They're both berry, that's all they had." She set the food and drink down close to Greg so he could reach them then pulled up a kitchen chair for herself.

"Why don't we eat first? Then we can spread the maps out on the coffee table," Jen suggested.

"Okay. Probably for the best. With my luck I'll get Thousand Island dressing right where we need to look."

Jen smiled as she produced two plastic forks from the deli bag. "I'd say your luck is pretty good," she said. "It was bad luck that your plane conked out but you could have been hurt a lot worse or even died."

Greg pursed his lips then nodded his head. "You're right, of course, but I could still get dressing on the map. I can be pretty sloppy, especially since I'm gimped up."

"So what have you been reading lately?" asked Jen as she settled back in her chair with her sandwich.

"I just finished a novel – fiction – about a DEA agent who was kidnapped in South America and rescued by an elite hostage rescue team. It was more of a tactical planning novel than a shoot-'em-up." he said.

"You read those a lot?"

"Oh, sometimes. I like to vary what I read so I don't wind up reading the same kind of stuff one right after the other. I like to read military history fiction but, again, not all at once. Another recent read was about the Roman centurion who was present when Christ was crucified and what happened to him. It was very interesting. What about you?"

"I like a variety too. I love to read adventures involving diving in the Florida keys for treasure but offset them with an occasional romance. Your Roman centurion sounds like something I'd be interested in reading."

"I liked it so much," said Greg, "that I bought the book. I'll loan it to you before you leave. Today I have been on the internet looking up stuff about our late prospectors."

"Oh? What did you find?"

"I found death certificates for Albert Neal, Josiah Carter and Micah Clapton but nothing for Jake Humbertson. My guess is that he was killed by Indians and his body never recovered. I also tried to trace the Yuma Bank and Trust. After several mergers it's now part of 1st Bank Yuma. I called about records and the clerk told me the records probably no longer existed but she'd call me back."

"I'd call the same person back in a couple of days. It has been my experience that most clerks have a fortress mentality. Most try to help you when you're on the phone but once you're off, the wall goes back up and they hide behind it. If you don't bug them, they never call back."

"That's what I figured. I had a helluva tough time getting her name and extension number but I did, and I'll call her back. It's almost like you have to fight with them to get the information. It doesn't cost them anything, why should they care about releasing it?"

"They get so many demands for their time that they can't keep up," said Jen. "That's why it's so important that someone like me cultivate specific contacts in various bureaucracies who get to know me and are willing to go the extra mile for me. It takes time to do that and that's what a client is paying for. It's all about rapport building whether it be a mutual love of dogs or a crappy boyfriend, we have something in common. It makes us friends and I'm not one of the enemy."

"Don't tell me you have a crappy boyfriend, I'd have to go beat some sense into him with my crutch!" Greg exclaimed.

Jen smiled. "That was just an example but no, I don't have a crappy boyfriend; as a matter of fact I don't have a boyfriend right now."

"Why not? I mean . . ." he added hastily, ". . . not why don't you have a crappy boyfriend but why no boyfriend?" He paused, then said, "I'm sorry, that's none of my business but you're so pretty with a personality to match, why aren't the guys chasing after you?"

"I don't mind the question," said Jen with a smile. "I don't have time right now for a boyfriend, and, frankly, the ones I've had lately seem a little lacking, if that makes any sense."

"I know exactly what you're saying; you could say I'm in the same boat. Well, I don't have the looks or personality you do but the girls I've been seeing – well, I guess I'm looking for something more."

Jen locked eyes with Greg for a moment and Greg felt a stronger jolt of adrenalin go through him.

Greg broke eye contact then glanced back at her. "I mean, I'm almost thirty and I'm tired of party girls. All they want to do is drink, hang out with their friends and party and occasionally get laid. I guess I'm growing out of the phase because now it bores me. There's no intellectual discourse, no discussion of the future and no plans but go to the next party. What kind of life is that?"

"I know," said Jen, nodding her head. "Seems like all the guys that I've been out with either want to get laid or talk about themselves. They seem to take everything else for granted and not to look to the future at all. I doubt any of them have read a book since they got out of school."

An awkward silence settled between them, both realizing they had let down their guard a little.

Both had finished their lunch so, to break the mood, Jen stood up and began to clear away the lunch debris. "I guess we'd better take a look at the maps," she said, "If I get my stuff back today, I'll go to Yuma tomorrow and poke around in some files. It would be useful if I knew where to poke."

"Did you get your car window fixed already?" Greg asked.

"The tape and plastic will do until I can take the time to have it done. It's a little noisy but not a big deal. Besides, I haven't called my insurance company to report it yet and I assume they'll want to come out and take a look at it. I need to go to Yuma more than I need to get it fixed."

"Why don't you take my Tahoe?" suggested Greg. "I'm pretty certain I'm not going to be using it. Tape and plastic have a way of breaking loose and when they do, there's an awful lot of noise and an unpleasant draft. The truck is even full of gas."

"Nah. I'd feel terrible if something happened to your car while I was using it. Besides, I'm used to my car, it'll be fine."

She picked up the bag from U of A and began pulling out maps. "I wasn't sure what to get this time so I just got a USGS map of the Growler Mountain area and the Growler Valley. I also got BLM maps of the same area and hoped it included where you found the saddlebags. Did I miss anything?"

"We're purely guessing that the claim is somewhere in the proximity of where the saddlebags were buried but it's as logical a place to start as any. I'd feel a lot better if we could find that darn seep. I suppose that's your first priority?"

"Actually, I'll just start with a simple name searches in

BLM's General Land Office files, pre-1908. The prospectors made a metes and bounds description instead of by section, township and range even though the public land survey system existed as far back as 1785. I'll be going through federal as well as state and local tract books. There are also deeds and plat maps to search and the Seven States Index. It's a name index to the pre-July 1908 general land entry case files, maintained on file cards. What's really good about this file is that it lists all successful land patents *and* unsuccessful land entries."

"Jeez, that sounds like a lot of checking," said Greg.

"That's only scratching the surface!" said Jen with a smile as she folded up the maps.

"At least now I know now where to start my searches."

CHAPTER 9

Unlike young Paco Gutierrez, Alfredo Menendez had hoarded his share of the proceeds from the smash and grab robberies. It wasn't that Alfredo was thrifty; he was trying to branch out in the criminal world. He was saving his money so he could buy several pounds of marijuana and thus break into the drug trade.

This untimely arrest – they all are, aren't they? – would force Alfredo to use his stash to hire a private attorney to defend himself. In Alfredo's opinion, the Public Defender (PD) assigned to his case was a snot-nosed kid who didn't know an affidavit from an indictment and both were in play here. To make it worse, Alfredo was out on recognizance for a similar case just six weeks old. He was worried about going to prison for a while and didn't like that idea at all. He didn't mind doing even a year in the county slam but frankly he was afraid of going to the big house.

He needed a good attorney, some gunslinger crafty in the ways of the courtroom and not afraid to exploit any advantage that might come their way, ethical or not. He had just the lawyer in mind: Jimbo McVey. McVey had been around a long time and was known for his *very* broad interpretation of the law. Put another way, Jimbo was a crook with no scruples or integrity and would win by whatever means he could. He was just the kind of lawyer who could get Alfredo's charges merged into one and a favorable plea deal arranged. After all, it was that ignorant moron, Paco, who got shot and opened his big mouth. If he had clammed up, Alfredo would have walked!

Alfredo had been before a judge once already but he knew the prosecutor's office would bring these four cases before a grand jury and Alfredo knew what that meant. His recognizance on the previous case had already been revoked so he was sitting in jail on that charge while the slow wheels of justice got ready to roll over him with four more indictments. He would be arraigned on the new charges and that's when Alfredo would have his PD inform the Court that Alfredo desired to hire a private attorney. The PD would arrange a meeting with Jimbo McVey and would then hopefully fade into the woodwork.

Alfredo knew he didn't have enough cash to pay for a high priced attorney like Jimbo McVey but he had something else and it would show up in the case discovery the prosecutor was obliged to give the defense. If Alfredo wasn't mistaken, those papers that Paco had stolen from the third victim spoke of a gold claim and there was a receipt for forty-two ounces of gold as well. *That* would get McVey's attention!

Two days later Alfredo was taken before a judge and arraigned on four counts of robbery in the first degree. At that time his PD announced that Mr. Menendez wanted to hire a private attorney and the PD withdrew.

Two days later, Jimbo McVey himself came to see Alfredo at the jail. As his name implied, Jimbo was a *big* man, big of girth but not of height. He wore a dark blue Brooks Brothers pinstriped suit, a white, custom tailored dress shirt and a regimental tie. He was florid and fleshy and smelled of expensive cologne. His piggy eyes missed nothing.

"Mr. Menendez," said Jimbo in a deep voice, "I was told that you wanted to see me – to hire me actually. You do realize that I don't do *pro bono* work, I'm too busy?"

"Yeah, I understand that and, to be honest, I don't have the cash to pay for your services but I might have something as good – *gold,* forty-two ounces of it and maybe more."

Jumbo's eyes narrowed, as they did when he smelled profit. "You have forty-two ounces of gold?"

"Well, not exactly, but I know where it is."

"And where is that?"

Alfredo had to be really careful here. If he told the attorney he only knew about the gold from the receipt from that girl's purse, he would leave without another word but if he could string him along, maybe he could convince the great Jimbo McVey to get him out of jail so he could go get the gold. Alfredo was pretty sure the bitch that Paco robbed before he was shot had the gold, and it would be a simple matter of breaking into her house and finding it if he could just get out of the slam.

"If I told you that," said Alfredo, "there wouldn't be any reason for you to represent me. You'd go get the gold or have someone get it for you and I'd still be in jail. It's not that I don't trust you, but this is business, I hope you understand."

"Conversely, how do I know there even is any gold?" asked McVey, his eyes narrowing further as they did when he was intensely analyzing a situation or a person.

"Do you really think a person like *me* would try to scam a person like *you?* I'm just a peon who has come across something valuable that is available for the taking and I mean to take it as soon as I get out of here. A big part of the proceeds could be yours if you can get me out of here; otherwise it stays where it is."

"I hope you believe what you're saying because if you were to fail, the repercussions could be severe."

Don't I know it! "It wouldn't necessarily be that tough to get me recogged," said Alfredo, ignoring the threat. "I wasn't even there when Paco broke the windows and I didn't see anything he stole until he handed it to me inside my car three blocks away. You could say I didn't know what he was doing until he showed up with the stuff."

"That may very well be," said Jimbo, caution tempering his words. "But I remain unconvinced that you can get your hands on … what you say you can. If you know where all this gold is, why are you out smashing and grabbing out of cars?"

This was the acid test; if Alfredo hesitated even for a second he was lost. The best lies have some truth in them. "I was saving it for a big score. I wanted to cop a couple of pounds of cola to start

68

with and get into the drug trade, there's real money to be made there."

"You could buy more than a couple of pounds of cocaine with forty-two ounces of gold," McVey observed.

"I know but I didn't want to spend it all at once in case something happened. You know?"

McVey nodded. "Prudent." He pondered for a few moments longer then made his decision. "Very well, I'll represent you. I hope, for your sake, you can deliver. It will cost you thirty-six ounces of gold."

"But that hardly leaves me with anything!" Alfredo protested.

"It leaves you out of jail, doesn't it?"

With Jimbo McVey running interference, it didn't take long for, Alfredo Menendez to walk out of the Pima County Jail a free man with nothing but a court date one month hence in his pocket. Behind his smile was a feeling of near desperation – he had to find out where the woman who had the papers lived so he could break into her house and steal the gold, *and* whatever he could find that would tell him the location of the gold claim. Jimbo McVey had given him a week to deliver thirty-six ounces of gold. Alfredo remembered clearly what the big man had repeated as they parted after the judge released Alfredo, "If you fail, the repercussions will be severe." Alfredo correctly took that to mean it would involve not only him but those close to him. That was the way the big man worked.

He racked his brain to think of a way to get the woman's name. The police would not release that information nor would Jimbo without his suspicions being aroused. Then he had it! The court! The affidavit supporting the search warrant for his home likely included the crime reports filed by the victims as exhibits to save the writer having to describe the crimes. After the search warrant was executed, the warrant, along with the affidavit had to be returned to the court. Unless the judge sealed the warrant, which was rare, the whole affidavit and warrant would be a public record! He would have to go to the courthouse and request a copy of the file and then he would have the information he needed. It took about an hour and a half from the time Alfredo entered the Pima County Courthouse for Alfredo to find the right court window and request a copy of the file. The clerk didn't bat an eye. Ironically, Alredo had to dip into his saved money from the robberies to pay the $37 copy fee, but finally he was in possession of the information he needed. The moment he got back in his car, he opened the envelope and began leafing through the pages: *Jenivive Karen Belle Isle, 1741 N. Campbell Avenue #1154, Tucson.* That was her, and the report said she was a self-employed public researcher. Obligingly, it provided a telephone number but also said that her work hours varied. That wasn't good, he didn't know when she would be home and he sure as hell didn't want to run into her in the apartment. It did, however, give a description of her car and its license number.

Alfredo chose to do some looking around before making his entry. 1741 N. Campbell Avenue was in a huge, modern apartment complex. It was a four-story building with apartment entrances on opposing sides. He was relieved to see that #1154 was a ground floor apartment and the entrance was screened from the public sidewalk by a six-foot-wall around a small courtyard. At this time of the day, about two in the afternoon, there weren't many cars in the parking lot, including the blue Honda Civic driven by Ms. Belle Isle.

He chose an unnumbered parking space where he could see the approach to her apartment from a distance, and settled down to wait for a while, just to get a feel for the activity in the neighborhood. It also gave him time to think and plan his next step. It wouldn't do to be impulsive and get caught busting into a house considering his current status. No one paid him any attention.

Cars started coming home at about 3:30 PM and the traffic continued until about 7:30 PM. Jenivive's car remained absent. Perhaps she was working late, maybe she had a date, or was getting her car's window fixed, who knew? All Alfredo knew was that he was hungry and his butt was asleep. At 8:00 PM, Alfredo started his car and pulled out of the complex parking lot. He would return in the morning early and see if she was home and maybe he'd get lucky and see her leave.

As he drove home, Alfredo debated the merits of a home invasion robbery, but he didn't have a gun and he wouldn't be very effective with his fist in a hoodie pocket! He didn't like guns and preferred not to have anything to do with them. Besides, if you got caught, having a weapon always made things worse – at least five years worse. He might have to resort to that if he didn't find what he was looking for when he broke in, probably tomorrow.

CHAPTER 10

Greg couldn't remember *ever* having such a good time with a woman as he had had with Jen. They worked and discussed the search for the Cactus Wren Claim for hours then shifted smoothly to talking about themselves. Jesse came home from work, forgetting that he was supposed to have gone to the grocery store. They told him not to worry about it and he immediately lit out for Susan's. Greg ordered Chinese take-out and he and Jen had dinner together.

They lounged comfortably in the living room. Greg had his leg stretched out on the couch on a pillow, and Jen relaxed on a love seat - an end table away. The maps had all been folded, and all the notes stowed. "Jen," Greg began as he put his water glass down on their common end table, "I gotta tell you, I have never been as comfortable talking to a woman as I am with you."

Jen smiled over her glass at her companion. "I was just thinking the same thing. The search for this claim should go so easily."

"I'll drink to that," said Greg as he raised his glass.

Jen did the same thing and reached over and clinked glasses with her host. She drained her glass then said, "I'd better be going. I have a tough boss and had better be to work on time in the morning or else."

Greg laughed. "I hate to see you go . . ." then stopped, hoping Jen would see past the *double entendre*. He struggled with his crutches to rise as Jen carried the glasses into the kitchen. When she returned, he was standing by the door.

She smiled as she picked up her purse from the love seat. "I had a terrific time tonight, too, Greg. Maybe when I get back from Yuma we can do it again."

"I'd like that," he said softly as she approached him at the door. There was no hesitation or awkwardness as she glided up against him and kissed him without hesitation. It was *not* a chaste peck on the lips and lasted several seconds.

"Whew!" gasped Greg, "Now I *really* hate to see you go."

She laughed. "You're hardly in a condition for *that*."

"Would that I was," he murmured then kissed her again. "How long do you think you'll be in Yuma?"

She backed up a step as he opened the door. "Not sure," she replied, "depends on what I find. Surely no more than a couple of days."

"Well, hurry back," he said and leaned in to kiss her once more. He stood at the door and watched her walk down the sidewalk until she turned a corner and was out of sight.

*****

The next morning, at about seven, Alfredo Menendez watched Jen load a briefcase, an overnight bag and her computer case into her Honda and drive away. He would wait until at least ten before making his entry since he didn't want to run into any neighbors on their way to work.

He was grateful for the privacy wall around most of the entrance, it made it easier to work without being noticed. Anticipating the need for accessories, Alfredo had brought a small bag of tools. He didn't want to kick in the front door because of the noise it would cause and looked for other options. The three-foot-wide door was steel with a steel jamb and he wasn't sure his tried and trusty pry bar would handle it. There was a narrow, decorative window next to the door and Alfredo recognized it as his target.

He paused and listened for at least five minutes then drew out a roll of duct tape. He tore off foot-long strips and applied them to the glass near the door latch. Finished, he replaced the roll in his bag then donned heavy leather gloves over his vinyl gloves and pulled a spring-loaded center punch from his bag. With a simple release of the trigger, he shattered the glass into fragments, but due to the tape, they remained in place. Alfredo gently pushed in on the taped section of glass. It flexed slightly then gave way and fell forward into the room leaving a hole about a foot square. He returned the center punch to his bag then raked the remaining glass pieces from the frame before reaching in to find the lock.

He located the manual dead bolt lock and turned it counter clockwise, unlocking the door. Alfredo quickly slipped inside the apartment with his bag then froze, his ears straining for any sounds as he returned his heavy gloves to his bag.

Still listening intently, he closed the door but did not re-lock it. Next he hurried to the back patio door and unlocked it, pulling it open a crack. Finally he made a cursory search of the apartment to ensure there were no people or dogs – either of whom could ruin his day. Finding neither, Alfredo entered the bedroom that appeared to be converted to an office.

Alfredo was never known as a neat burglar and he lived up to his reputation in Jen's apartment. With desperate recklessness, he went through first the office, then the other rooms in the apartment like a small tornado, pulling out and emptying drawers, pulling books off bookshelves and generally leaving the place a discouraging mess. He searched frantically since he was constantly aware that Jimbo McVey was always lurking in the shadows of his mind, waiting.

Finally there was no place else to look. He had found nothing. He stumbled through the debris of the apartment one more time – with the same results. But he was sure he had seen a receipt for forty-two ounces of gold! She must have stashed it in her car or had it in a safe deposit box or something. Either that or she was carrying it with her. Regardless, his next step was obvious, he would have to brace her face to face. As a rule, he wasn't the type to hurt women but he might have to in this case. It was either her or him and Alfredo had no illusions about what would befall him if Jimbo or his people got hold of him.

Judging by her luggage, the bitch probably wouldn't be home tonight. She was either out of town or shacked up with some asshole of a boyfriend. Now he was sorry he had made such a mess of her apartment. She would *not* be appreciative and that would make her far less willing to talk to him. Tough. She'd talk.

*****

Completely oblivious to the havoc wreaked at her apartment, Jen had arrived in Yuma and was debating going directly to the BLM Field Office or checking into a motel and using its Wi-Fi to search for records pertaining to the Cactus Wren Claim and its entryman, Jake Humbertson, the entryman being the individual who actually filed the mining claim.

She knew she needed to search the pre-1908 patented and unpatented general land entry files of BLM's predecessor, the General Land Office. She decided to go to BLM first and search the Seven States Index which listed the pre-1908 named claimants in seven states including Arizona.

Jen began searching for Jake Humbertson's name in the Seven States Index. She was hopeful Humbertson's name would pop up, and it did! Unfortunately, the file showed no more information than the receipt Greg had found in the saddlebag and there would be no subsequent files since there was no section, township and range. Jen was disappointed, she had hoped the clerk had had Humbertson point out the location of the claim on a map so the clerk could determine at least a township and range but there were no such entries.

To be thorough, Jen also ran the names of Humbertson's partners through the index, and was surprised to find that Micah Clapton had three other claims, dated earlier than the Cactus Wren claim. She examined them closely to see if there was any clue to their physical location but all were metes and bounds surveys with innocuous landmarks that did not include a seep. None had ever been patented.

Jen ran all four names and the name of the claim through a variety of state and federal mining files and records searching for one little notation in a margin that would be the clue to finding the physical site since it wasn't listed anywhere by township and range. When she finished, she found herself empty-handed, hungry and tired, then realized she had worked straight through the noon hour and it was now mid-afternoon.

She went out for a late lunch, then returned to BLM to search for any pre-1908 general land entry file indices she might have missed. She found nothing she hadn't seen before so she shifted over to Yuma and Pima Counties and made the same searches . . . with the same results except this time Jake Humbertson and Micah Clapton did not appear.

A little discouraged, Jen went out for a late dinner then returned to her room. From experience she knew that a search like this was akin to searching for the proverbial needle in the haystack. More than once, when she had been close to giving up on a search, the much-sought-after clue would miraculously appear. This time she was more determined than usual, and wondered if that had to do with Greg Miller.

That she was taken with him was a given, they had so much in common! She liked that he was in a set career and clearly had a set of values that was near her own. *And* he had made it clear that he was attracted to her. She decided to call him, ostensibly to give him an update on her search.

"Hello?"

"Hi Greg, this is Jen."

"Hey. How are you doing? It's good to hear from you even though it hasn't even been twenty-four hours."

"I know. I thought you'd like to know about the research."

"That too but I'm just glad to hear from you. Believe it or not I've been expecting your call for about an hour. What took you so long?"

"Are you psychic or something?" she asked with a laugh.

"Well, maybe a little psycho, but a lot hopeful. Does that make sense?"

"Not exactly but I'm glad to hear it anyway. I'm in Yuma and have been in front of a computer or microfilm screen all day. I found Jake Humbertson in a pre-1908 file but it didn't give any more information than your claim receipt. Micah Clapton had three other claims but there's no way to connect them with the information the files provide."

"I guess that's not too much of a surprise," said Greg.

"Clapton's claims might be right next to the Cactus Wren and we'd never know based on the metes and bounds survey landmarks instead of township and range. Yuma County was established in the same year as Pima County, 1864, so I did the same searches in Pima County as I did in Yuma."

"Sounds like you've been hard at it, anything I can do to help?" asked Greg. "After all, I'm just sitting here on my butt watching a shadow crawl across the ceiling."

"Don't you have any good books to read?"

"Yeah, but with the prescriptions I'm taking, it's almost impossible to concentrate on the print."

"How about an audio book on your phone?"

"Hadn't thought of that; then again, I'd have no idea how to go about buying one."

"I'll show you when I get back, even I can do it."

"Thank you . . . I think. By then, hopefully, I'll be off the pain killers and that's what's doing it to me."

"How does your knee feel?"

"It doesn't hurt as much today but it feels like it's the size of a basketball."

"You'd better get over that quickly, you may have to trudge up and down mountains to find that gold claim."

"Luckily, it's a placer claim so we don't have to blast and haul rocks out. Digging up gravel and debris is bad enough from what I hear."

"I don't know anything about placer mining – or lode mining for that matter. I always assumed it was hard, dirty work judging from the photographs I've seen of the California Forty-Niners and such."

"I don't either," Greg admitted, "but that's why Jesse agreed to go work with a prospector for a while."

"Has he made any progress in finding one?"

"I've hardly seen Jesse since the crash. He's been flying a lot, I know that, and spending his time with Susan."

"Are you able to manage without him?"

"Oh yeah. He brought in a bunch of groceries before he had to go to work this morning. He'll be here to drive me when I have a doctor's appointment and mostly I can get along fine without any help."

"I don't know about that; I may have to come over more often just to keep an eye on you."

"In that case I may be in a bad way and will need a lot of assistance to get me through all these trying times," Greg cried piteously.

"You really are full of it, aren't you, Miller?" Jen said with a giggle. "I may come home tomorrow if I can get to see the files I need early enough. I'll let you know."

"I'll be here," said Greg cheerfully. "You just be careful on the highways, okay?"

"Yes, dad." With that, she hung up with a smile on her face.

CHAPTER 11

By eleven the next morning, in search of the Ahren's Seep, Jen was so rummy from poring over government bureaucratic documents having to do with water ways that she was numb. There were *so* many agencies, committees and task forces involved in the preservation of the natural resources of the Barry M. Goldwater Range and the Cabeza Prieta Wildlife Refuge to the south of the range, her head was spinning. The best she had found was a map of the BMGR showing the known tinajas and what kinds of animals drank there.

She stopped long enough for a cup of coffee and a sandwich, then decided that she could just as easily wade through this stuff at home as in Yuma. Besides, she wanted to see Greg. She had already checked out of her motel room and thus only had to gather up her computer, pads and pens and head for her car. Three and a half hours later she was back in Tucson and pulling into a parking spot at Greg's apartment complex.

She had one quick moment of indecision then decided to go ahead. The worst that could happen was that she found him in the shower or asleep. With his knee, he'd better not be in the shower!

She knocked on the door and heard him say, "It's open."

She found him sleepy-eyed on the couch looking *good* in a pair of gym shorts and an Air Force t-shirt. When he saw who it was, he grinned widely. "Welcome back!" he said as he half-rose from the couch.

"Oh, stay put," she admonished. "You don't have to get up for me. How are you feeling?"

"Okay," he replied. "Bored silly. Please say you have something for me to do!"

She considered his question and thought of what she had

been doing all morning and nodded. "I hope you have lots of patience. I've been going through reams of bureaucratic nonsense in search of Ahren's Seep and have barely scratched the surface. Wanna help?"

Greg smiled again and said, "You bet. Can you stay and work with me?"

She nodded. "All I need is an electrical plug-in and a little room to spread out my note-taking materials."

"Well, pull the love seat over to the coffee table. There's electricity behind this end table. Gee, I'm really glad to see you. How was your trip?"

"Not very productive. The best thing was finding Jake Humbertson's name in the Seven States Index. After doing all the name searches, I've gone on to waterways trying to track down Ahren's Seep. I do know that there are a number of tinajas on the BMGR and the Cabeza Prieta Wildlife Refuge – too many to search even if we could get to them."

"You know, of course, that what we propose to do if we find the claim is illegal on either reservation?"

"Uh huh. That became apparent early on."

"I figured we'd cross that bridge when we came to it *if* we ever got that far."

"Yeah," Jen said, "there are a lot of ifs standing in our way right now but my focus remains on finding the damned claim. I'd like you to concentrate on the name of the seep on the internet while I chase after the tinajas. I'm thinking that maybe someone will slip and mention Ahren's seep in connection with a particular tinaja or," she said, motioning toward Greg, "the opposite."

They worked until seven when Jen called a halt. "I've had enough," she said, clicking her laptop closed. "When did you eat last?"

"I had lunch," Greg replied defensively.

"Yeah, I'll bet you did. Peanut butter and jelly?"

"Peanut butter has protein in it," said Greg, a little

defensively.

Exasperated, Jen said, "Okay, fine. Is there anything here I can make dinner out of or do we need to order out?"

Greg looked downright sheepish. "What?" Jen asked. "Didn't Jesse just go to the store?"

"Yeah. But neither of us cook much so he got some microwavable dinners and sandwich stuff."

"Okay, we'll order something – *you* buy while I make a list for Jesse so I can at least fix a decent dinner tomorrow. Okay?"

Looking relieved, Greg nodded. Jen then gave Greg the phone number of a good Mexican restaurant that delivered, then went to work on a *real* list for Jesse. She finished at about the time the food arrived and they ate mostly in companionable silence. When they finished and Jen had cleaned up, she plopped down on the couch next to Greg. He had shifted his leg onto the coffee table with his knee slightly bent. Unconsciously he rubbed the badly bruised quadriceps above the brace on his injured knee.

Jen leaned over toward him and put her hand on his hand, as he was rubbing his injured leg. "Pretty sore, huh?" she asked.

He shrugged and stopped rubbing but she didn't remove her hand. He looked down at their joined hands then up into her eyes. He smiled a small, slow smile then leaned over and kissed her. "I've wanted to do that since you left the other night," he murmured.

"Seems to me you did a pretty good job of it before I left," she remarked, a slight smirk on her face. "Why don't you try again and we'll see if practicing has helped."

"Was it that bad?" he asked, sticking his lower lip out.

Jen rubbed her thumb across his lower lip as she stared into his eyes, then leaned in for a much more passionate kiss that lasted several seconds. His lips wandered to her earlobe then to her neck and her response was a deep intake of breath.

"It grieves me to report that this is as far as I can manage at this time," he whispered against her ear.

"It grieves me to hear it, but I do understand," she whispered back.

"I feel like I'm back in high school and afraid your parents might catch us. That's not what I had in mind," he said, again in a soft voice.

"Me neither," she whispered, rubbing his leg above the knee. "But you don't have to worry about Mom and Dad, they won't be home for hours. Besides, I'm a good girl and won't let you go too far."

"Damn it!" Greg cried in mock despair.

"I know, baby, I know. Maybe I should go, I don't want to get you all upset."

"But I don't want you to go," he protested.

"And I'd much rather stay, but you're already in a dither."

"No, I'm not!"

She gently squeezed his erection as she said, "I don't believe you. But I haven't even been home yet, I drove straight here from Yuma. I'll be back tomorrow. As a matter of fact, if Jesse fills that list at the store, I'll cook you breakfast."

That mollified him a little, but his heart was still set on her staying. She gave him one more kiss then stood up. "Can I come back tomorrow?" she asked, smiling at him.

"Absolutely," he said, dejected, "the earlier the better." She retrieved her purse and left . . . leaving Greg feeling all alone.

In more of a dither herself than she wanted to admit to Greg, Jen drove home. She parked in her assigned spot, gathered up her purse, computer case and overnight bag then walked up the sidewalk toward her apartment. She didn't notice the shattered window with a hole in it. The first inkling she had of trouble was when her shoes crunched on the broken glass inside the door. She switched on a light and when she saw the devastation that was her living room, she froze then started to back out of the apartment.

Suddenly an arm snaked around her waist and a knife was

pressed against her neck. "Hey mama, where you goin'? Don' run off, we need to talk," said a man's voice with a distinct Latino accent.

Jen stiffened and stood frozen, afraid to move.

The man's body nudged her back into the apartment until he could close the door behind them. "Okay, jus' ease over to the sofa and sit," he ordered, the blade still firmly pressed against Jen's neck. They shuffled over to the sofa and the man pushed Jen down. He kept his legs pressed against the front of her legs to keep her from getting back up. He held the blade in his hand, down by his side.

"Now gringa, we talk," he said triumphantly.

"Who are you? What do you want? I have no money so ..."

"Silencio (shut up)!" Alfredo thundered. He wasn't used to assertive women and he didn't like it one bit. "You will sit there and listen and speak only to answer my questions."

Jen was gritting her teeth doing a slow burn, her fear quickly supplanted by anger. But she held her tongue, at least until she found out what the intruder was after.

Alfredo didn't beat around the bush, "You have gold, I want it. Where is it?"

"Gold?" Jen questioned. "What makes you think I have any gold? I don't have any gold except a few pieces of cheap jewelry."

"Don't lie to me, you bitch!" Alfredo all but screamed. "I have proof. You will tell me where the gold is or . . ." he said, waving the knife, ". . . or you will die!"

"I don't have any gold!" Jen yelled. "Whoever told you that is lying . . ." Then it came to her in a flash, "You! You tore my place apart! Did you find any? No! Because I don't have any gold!"

"Then you have it in the bank," Alfredo accused, concern that he might be wrong oozing into his head. "There was a receipt from a bank. Forty-two ounces of gold. You will go get it and give it to me or I will kill you! I will cut off your head!"

Finally it made sense to Jen. This asshole was connected to

the man who had robbed her, he had seen the receipt stolen from her and decided she had the gold, not noticing the 1889 date on the receipt from the Yuma Bank and Trust

"You've made a mistake," she said, more calmly. "The receipt you saw was dated May of 1889, one hundred thirty-two years ago. The gold is long gone, taken by the State of Arizona. It's called escheatment – if no one claims the gold, it eventually goes to the state."

"This cannot be! I saw the receipt myself."

"I can prove it to you," said Jen. "Just let me get into my computer case and I'll show you a copy of the receipt." Alfredo backed away from Jen and she stood up. She went to her computer case, rummaged through the loose papers and handed one to her captor.

Alfredo read through it quickly, noting the May 20, 1889, date. "This cannot be," he moaned, more to himself than Jen, "Jimbo will have me killed for this."

"Who's Jimbo? Jen asked.

"That is none of your business," Alfredo snapped. Then, in a moment of inspiration, he asked, waving the receipt at Jen, "Where did you get this?"

It was Jen's turn to be evasive. "And *that's* none of your business."

He glared at her as he snarled, "It is my business if I say it is. Where did it come from?" He brandished the knife at her.

She stood there looking defiantly at him until his hand whipped out like a whipsnake and backhanded her across the face, making her nose bleed. "Do not think for a moment that I won't use violence to get what I want."

Jen tried to stanch the flow of blood with her fingers then pulled a tissue from her pocket and held it against her nose.

"I got it from a friend who asked me to check on it. I found that it is too old, the gold has been turned over to the state and there's no record that I can find of the man who deposited the gold. It's a dead end."

"You are lying to me."

"No I'm not. Check into it yourself, you'll see."

Alfredo glanced at Jen's computer bag. "What else do you have in there?"

"Nothing that would interest you."

"Perhaps . . ." Alfredo said as he snatched the bag from Jen, "... I'll see for myself."

Jen fought to keep the bag but he was too strong and again brandished the knife at her. He riffled through some of the papers then looked up at her.

"I'll kill you if you're lying to me, bitch," he snarled as he stuffed the papers back in the computer case. "I'll just take this with me. Go sit on the sofa, NOW!" As she turned to walk back to the sofa, Alfredo quietly slipped out the front door before Jen was even aware he was gone. When she discovered his absence she collapsed on the sofa, broke into tears and covered her face with her hands. She didn't cry for long before anger took over. Alfredo had left her purse which she grabbed and rooted around until she found her phone. She immediately called 911 and reported the burglary and subsequent assault and robbery. Finished with the call, she started to call Greg but hesitated. If she told him, he would do everything he could, including mess up his knee to come to her. She decided that she would wait until the police had done their investigation then she would drive over to Greg and Jesse's.

CHAPTER 12

Alfredo walked deliberately away from Jen's apartment but didn't run back to his car – that would call attention to himself. He drove away from the neighborhood to a busy Walmart and parked his car in among several others. The store, as usual was busy and no one paid him any heed.

He unzipped the side pocket of the computer case, took out the small sheaf of papers and began to read them, first the letter from Albert Neal to Jake Humbertson, then the rest of the papers pertaining to the claim. He stared out the windshield. *How can these papers save my life with Jimbo McVey?* Alfredo knew that the only chance he had of staying alive was to go to McVey and hope the big man would give him time to explain.

If he tried to avoid McVey around town, or even leave Tucson, his life would be forfeit if he was ever caught. There was no one he could go to borrow seventy or eighty thousand dollars and if he could, it would just be delaying the inevitable with some other crime boss. He had to use the papers to buy some time. If McVey would give him, say, a month, he was sure he could come up with the location of the gold claim. That bitch was the key and he was sure she was working with someone else. He had to find out who.

He thought of his wife and what she would do without him. She had no skills to make her way in the gringo world and would have to take the three kids and move back to Mexico. That would break her heart; she had lived here her whole life though she was born in Mexico. Alfredo was born in the U.S. which made him a citizen but Maria was always too shy to apply for citizenship, and feared she would be deported and separated from her three children forever.

Jimbo McVey was not known for being merciful but he

might listen if there was money to be made. If Alfredo could just get him interested in the claim . . .

It was time to face the lawyer. Alfredo drove downtown and found a parking space in the parking garage next to McVey's office building. He took the elevator up to the twelfth floor and, like a man going to his hanging, walked down the hall and into the law office. It was plush with deep pile carpeting, original paintings on the wall and real wood furniture. He walked up to the receptionist, self-conscious due to his appearance. Gang tats and clothing didn't really belong in a law office. Compared to her, he was dressed like a bum off the street.

"Can I help you?" she asked, haughty without words.

"Yeah, uh, I need to see Mr. McVey."

"Do you have an appointment, Mr. . . . ."

"I don't have an appointment but he'll want to see me. My name is Menendez, Alfredo Menendez."

"I'm afraid Mr. McVey is in court. Can I give him a message or would you like to make an appointment?"

"No, ah, yeah. Just let him know I came to see him and that it's really important I see him. See him, not talk to him on the phone."

"Does he have your phone number?"

Alfredo gave her his cell phone number. She looked at him and smirked, dismissing him with her eyes.

Alfredo shambled out of the office and took the elevator down to street level. McVey would find him, Alfredo was sure of that. He debated finding a coffee shop nearby and waiting for the call. He finally decided to go home. It might be the last time he got to see his family. He couldn't believe how relieved he felt just missing Jimbo McVey at the office! He knew he was only delaying his fate but at least he could see his wife and kids one more time.

*****

Jen was beyond bored. A whole gaggle of Tucson PD officers responded to her call and now, three hours later, most of them were still here. The Victim's Assistant, a young civilian woman, fawned over her and almost insisted that Jen go to the hospital to make sure her bloody nose wasn't broken. It was just a bloody nose, her eyes probably wouldn't even blacken.

She had been interviewed by no less than three detectives and was waiting for someone to come back with something called a throw down. She wasn't sure, but thought it had something to do with pictures, not guns like in the movies. She wanted to leave but that wasn't what the lead detective wanted, so she stayed. She had called Greg and talked him out of coming over, promising to go there no matter what the hour.

Finally a younger detective arrived with a folder. He explained that the folder might or might not have a photo of the man who robbed and assaulted her. He wanted her to take a long, slow look at all six photos and tell him if she saw the suspect among them.

It took Jen all of two seconds to recognize her assailant but she said nothing until she had examined each photograph carefully. When she finished with her examination, she pointed to the man in the number four position and declared positively that he was the man who had robbed and backhanded her. At the detective's request she circled his photograph and signed her name. She wasn't told that the procedure was merely a formality. When she told them the man had been somehow involved in the original robbery, they automatically went to Alfredo Menendez's photo and viola! a positive identification.

Finally even Tucson PD had had enough and cleared out, leaving the apartment black with fingerprint powder and in more disarray than Alfredo had left it. The victim's assistant stayed and helped her put things back in some semblance of order so when she left to go to Greg's, she wouldn't come home to a complete disaster.

It was after one in the morning when Jen knocked softly at Greg's door. She heard a muffled "It's open," and let herself in. He was lying on the couch with his right knee elevated and looked to be about half asleep. When he saw her he broke into a big grin and said, "You made it!"

He suddenly winced as he swung his injured leg onto the coffee table to give her room to sit down. He patted the cushion next to him and she dropped her purse on the other end of the couch then snuggled up next to him. "God, I've been looking forward to this!" she sighed.

"Me too," said Greg as he put his arm around her shoulders and just held her close. Finally he asked, "Do you want to talk about it?"

"Not tonight. I just want to be somewhere safe." Not much time elapsed before Greg detected the regular rhythm of her breathing and soon he joined her in slumber.

Jesse woke them both up at 6:30 A.M., when he came in loaded with groceries. "Mornin'" he said as he traipsed into the kitchen, loaded with plastic bags. He unloaded the bags on the kitchen counter then came back to the entrance into the living room. "I see y'all had a wild, passionate night."

"Yep, that's what we had alright," said Greg. "Jen was robbed again, this time at her apartment."

"He took my computer, my notes and all the claim papers," Jen added. "The police know who he is, they showed me a picture of him. They said he was working with the guy who broke my car window. They were looking for him and even checked his house again."

"Damnation, are they ever going to leave y'all alone?"

"He came for the forty-two ounces of gold; when I explained it was long gone, he got mad, backhanded me and threatened to cut my head off." "He found the other claim papers in my notes then took them and my computer and left. I doubt I've seen the last of him unless the police catch him."

"Was he armed?"

"He held a knife to my throat when he first came in, and waved it at me a few times but I wasn't cut."

"And the cops know who he is?" asked Jesse.

"Yeah, he was the other half of the team that broke the window on my car and stole the papers to begin with. They recovered my purse, the papers and stuff at his house, but wouldn't tell me where he lived, just someplace in South Tucson."

"Well, it's a lead pipe cinch you're not going to be staying in your apartment, at least until he's caught," said Greg grimly. "You can stay here, use Jesse's room; he's never here except when I need him."

Jesse nodded in agreement. "That would be more comfortable than sleeping next to Greg on the couch."

Jen sat up, turned and looked at Greg. "Oh I don't know," she said with a smile, "I sort of liked it."

"There's no accountin' for taste, I reckon," said Jesse, rolling his eyes. "We can go over there right now if y'all want, and get your stuff."

Jen stood up, walked around the end of the coffee table opposite Greg's injured knee, grabbed her purse, and headed for the bathroom. "I'll only be a minute," she said as she disappeared down the hall.

"I'm worried they aren't done with her," said Greg.

"They?"

"This asshole can't be working alone. If he was, he wouldn't have left. It looks to me like he's going for instructions; he doesn't know what to do next."

"What I'd do is grab her and, one way or another, get the whole story outta of her. If the cops were worth a shit, they'd have figured that out and put a guard on her," said Jesse, his mouth grim.

"That job falls to me," said Greg.

"Yeah, you're in great shape to protect someone."

"It doesn't take two legs to use my .40 caliber equalizer. If someone tries the same thing here, they'll wish they hadn't."

"A true Texas welcome," said Jesse with a grin. He paused then went into his bedroom and was in there long enough for Greg to start wondering what he was doing. Finally he emerged, a semi-automatic handgun nestled against his right side in a belt holster. "Open carry's legal in Arizona," was all he said.

Jen came out of the bathroom looking refreshed but stopped at the entrance to the living room when she saw Jesse was carrying a weapon. "Do you think that's necessary?" she asked.

"Do you think it's not?" asked Jesse and Greg simultaneously.

"No," Jen replied promptly, "I just wish I had one too."

"We'll see about that bye and bye," said Jesse. "Right now, let's go get your stuff."

They drove over to Jen's apartment and she looked at the broken window next to the door. She immediately got on her phone and called a glass company. To her surprise, they could come out immediately. She checked through the apartment to make sure no one had taken advantage of the compromised entryway to help themselves. To her relief, all appeared in order, relatively speaking.

Jen started packing clothes and toiletries while Jesse looked in the refrigerator to see what was perishable and what was safe to leave. Jen didn't know how long she'd be gone so she packed for the long term. She was grateful she worked for herself and didn't have a strict schedule to keep.

"I can't figure out how the crook knew I was just getting home. I mean, I literally had just unlocked the door and stepped inside when he came up behind me. I can't believe that any of my neighbors might be involved."

Jesse thought for a moment then said, "I don't want to scare y'all any worse than you've already been scared, but the guy was probably watching your apartment, waiting for you to come home.

And it's possible he might try to follow you away from here to see where you go. You should get in the habit of noticing what cars are behind you and if you're suspicious, try a couple of tricks like pulling over suddenly or turning a corner then parking, to see if they stay behind or try to go around you. This guy seemed pretty serious and doesn't sound like the type to give up easily."

"That does scare me, and my first inclination is to buy a gun. Any ideas?" asked Jen.

"I checked, and found that Arizona is an extremely friendly gun-owning state and that you don't need a permit to carry openly like I'm doing, or concealed. If you buy a gun it is incumbent on you to learn how to handle it safely and be familiar with the laws about its use. I think it's a good idea for you to get one. After all, the police officer who caught your robbers would have been just another victim had she not had a gun."

"Do you think Greg would be upset if we went gun shopping today?"

"I think Greg is mature enough to recognize your legitimate need for a gun and the fact that he's not able at this time to help you buy one. Call him if you want."

Jen liked that idea and got on her cell phone and called Greg. As expected, he was all for it. "Just don't bring home anything bigger than a .40 caliber, my fragile ego couldn't take that!"

After exhaustive searching – not unlike shopping for shoes – en chose a Smith & Wesson Bodyguard .380. She liked the way it fit in her hand and it wasn't so heavy she couldn't hold it up to aim. She also bought a holster and decided that the two magazines that came with it were sufficient.

The gun dealer did the required records checks over the phone and sold her the weapon plus two boxes of ammunition. She enrolled in a gun safety and concealed carry class and walked out of the store a happy girl.

Jesse and Jen hauled the boxes of possessions into Jesse and

Greg's apartment and she set about moving into Jesse's room amid his assurances that Susan had wanted him to move in with her for over a month. Greg sat on the couch with his leg up and a big grin on his face and watched them carry stuff in.

When they were done, they called Susan over and had a serious discussion about safety and security. As long as he was laid up, Greg would always have his .40 caliber Glock at arm's length and Jen would have her little .380 with her whenever she left the apartment. They agreed the potential for danger was higher but they wouldn't be caught flat-footed again. It was Jesse who thought of adding a few verbal signals and physical signs in case one of them was under duress.

CHAPTER 13

Not wanting to be caught at home by Jimbo McVey's henchmen thus endangering his family, Alfredo left after a couple of hours and drove over to one of his favorite hangouts, the Spot Tavern in South Tucson. He expected to be grabbed at any minute and hustled roughly into McVey's presence. His hope that the lawyer would call him faded with the afternoon sunshine. He ordered a Corona then took a seat at a dark, back table where he could see everything and no one could walk up behind him. He didn't know what else to do but wait. He would be summoned at the time and in the manner of Jimbo McVey's choosing and not before. He thought of looking on the bitch's computer but didn't know anything about them so he left it in the car. He kept the claim papers close, just in case.

A few minutes past six, Jimbo's men came for him. There were two of them and Alfredo had little doubt they were muscle, merely by the way they walked directly to his table and looked at him like a hungry coyote looks at a rabbit. Both wore sport coats over slacks to hide the bulge of shoulder holsters under their left armpits.

"Jimbo wants you," said one of the men, his voice raspy as if he had been a smoker a long time or had suffered trauma to his pharynx. Alfredo didn't even try to finish his beer but got up and waited for the rough stuff – which never came. They followed him out of the Spot where he hesitated, waiting for a beating or at least some indication which car they would take him in.

"What?" asked Raspy Voice.

"Which car?" asked Alfredo.

"Follow us in your own damned car," said the other thug, "we're not chauffeurs."

They didn't know how much hope those words gave Alfredo! Always staying close behind so as not to arouse any suspicions he had thoughts of running, Alfredo followed the men to a warehouse not far from the Spot. It was older, run down, with many broken windows. *A perfect place for a murder.*

They stopped, he stopped. They got out, so did he, waiting for instructions. Raspy Voice gestured toward the man door set in the front of the building and they all walked toward it, Raspy Voice in front of Alfredo, the other tagging along behind, close behind. Raspy Voice unlocked the door with a key and they entered. The warehouse stretched out before them huge and full of boxes and crates. Raspy Voice turned suddenly and told Alfredo to raise his arms. The hired killer searched Alfredo thoroughly for weapons and body wires before turning back around and leading them through a maze of alleyways of freight to the back. They climbed a set of wooden stairs to a second-story loft enclosed into an office. Raspy Voice knocked on the door and a muffled voice from inside bade them enter.

Alfredo couldn't stop shaking and had begun to sweat. He knew he was just moments away from peeing his pants when he stopped before the big man's desk. Raspy Voice lounged near the entrance door while the other thug took a position against a file cabinet within an arm's length of Alfredo. Jimbo McVey made no effort to calm Alfredo, he wanted the man to sweat. "You wanted to see me, so here I am." Before Alfredo could respond, McVey asked the thug nearest to them, "Has he been searched?" The man nodded. McVey turned back to Alfredo and said, "So? Where's my gold?"

It all came out of Alfredo in a rush. He was afraid he was making no sense when he pulled out the claim papers and dropped them on the desk before the big man.

McVey looked at the pages with distaste, they were wrinkled, creased and sweat-stained. "I already know all this," McVey said. "I got copies of all this in your case discovery yesterday."

"I'm sorry, Mr. McVey, I didn't even notice the date on that receipt until the bitch who had it called it to my attention. She said the forty-two ounces was long gone and insisted she had no gold. I believe her. I searched her apartment before she came home and her luggage after she did and found nothing."

"The gold *is* gone, to the state probably even before Arizona was a state. What I found of interest was the receipt for a placer mining claim referred to in the letter from Albert Neal to Jake Humbertson. It suggests there was a lot more gold. I don't suppose you and the lady discussed that, did you?"

"No. There was a lot of shouting going on and I had to smack her once so I figured it was time to leave. But I know where she lives, she won't be that hard to find. I'm sure she's working with someone else, and I thought finding out who they were and where was more important than going back to jail."

McVey sat there staring at Alfredo so long, he started to get edgy all over again. He had tried to make himself look as good as he could throughout this situation but he wasn't sure he had made much progress considering Mr. McVey's silence. Alfredo didn't notice McVey's subtle nod to the closest thug and was taken completely by surprise when the thug spun him around and buried his fist in Alfredo's solar plexus. Alfredo collapsed to his knees, his arms covering his stomach.

As Alfredo fought desperately to take a breath, McVey said, "I don't like people who cross me, usually they wind up dead. The only reason you're not is because you didn't try to run and came to me and told me the truth. Your status of remaining alive will change if you fuck up again. You go find that gold claim, I want it. Now take these papers and get out of my sight."

With the assistance of the goon who slugged him, Alfredo struggled to his feet. He still couldn't take a breath but was taking in enough air to know that if he remained one second longer, Mr. McVey might change his mind. He staggered to the door which was opened by Raspy Voice and closed behind him.

As he struggled down the stairs with a death grip on the rail, Alfredo still couldn't take a full breath but it was getting better; he was just grateful to be out of McVey's presence. He blindly made his way away from the office through the jungle of cargo, getting lost several times before finding the door. He staggered to his car and drove away not paying any attention to where he was going, just *away* from Jimbo McVey.

Alfredo finally got his breathing under control after he parked in the shade of a mesquite tree. He was able to breathe more-or-less normally but it really hurt in the area in which the goon had slugged him. He wondered if he had internal injuries and debated going to a hospital. He decided to wait a little while to see if the pain subsided. He wished he had a joint to ease the pain a little.

How in hell was he going to learn where the gold claim was? His only connection to it was the girl and he knew there was no way she would cooperate. Besides, she had probably gone to her partners and was even now planning a defense against him since it was obvious he needed information from her.

He would have to watch her apartment and follow anyone who showed up there. He should probably get another car in case she had noticed his Chevy. He thought of 'jacking one but decided it would be better to have a cool car so he went to his friend's tow company lot to see what he had available. The owner owed Alfredo a few favors and this would be a good way to settle the debt.

Alfredo had also decided to acquire a gun. After all, this time he wasn't pussyfooting around. Success in this caper probably meant that he would live; failure meant death, no probably about it. In all his other crimes, with people like Paco Gutierrez, people walked away unscathed more-or-less but this was different. If he was going to be in a life or death situation, so should the victims.

The knife hadn't really had much impact on Jen, but he was sure a round from a 9mm through the roof would get her attention. He didn't like guns, as a rule, but in this case, one was called for. The penalty for having a gun was higher but that didn't matter. If he failed, he died.

The owner of the tow lot was a trusted associate, both were

confident that the other wouldn't give him up if cornered. The owner had two weapons to choose from. The first was a Colt .38 special revolver which Alfredo rejected immediately; he wanted to be able to reload quickly with a full magazine. The other was an old Kel-Tec .380 with a rust-pitted barrel. It came with an extra magazine and both were loaded.

"Does it shoot?" asked Alfredo.

"Of course it shoots," said the owner, "I just can't vouch for its accuracy past twenty feet, it only has a two and a half inch barrel."

"That's okay as long as it fires," said Alfredo, hoping he'd never have to shoot anyone.

"I put a clip through it myself, shoots fine. Even cleaned it. It's a little rough on the outside but it's what's inside that counts, right?"

"Is it hot?"

"No idea, I found it in one of the cars I towed in, no one has ever asked about it."

"How much?" asked Alfredo.

"Oh hell, just take the damned thing. Just don't bring anything down on me with it."

"You know I'd never do that. Thanks man, 'preciate it and the use of the car." He was also appreciative that the man asked no questions.

Alfredo was still ambivalent about carrying a gun. On one hand he knew he needed one, but it really upped the ante on what could happen if he got caught. To be on the safe side, he took the weapon out into the desert and fired off a couple of rounds. It hardly kicked but it was loud as hell; he'd have to remember that. He tucked it into his jacket pocket along with the extra magazine and drove back home.

His wife was just feeding dinner to the children and he

decided to join them. He thought about earlier in the afternoon when he wasn't sure he'd ever see them again. He had to find that gold claim!

CHAPTER 14

After she closed and locked the door behind the departing Susan and Jesse, Jen walked over and sat down beside Greg on the couch. "What sounds good for dinner?" she asked.

"What's available?" asked Greg wishing more than ever that he wasn't crippled up.

"Well, let's see. There's chicken, hamburger, steak and even hot dogs. Anything sound good?"

"I don't suppose we could have spaghetti?" Greg asked hopefully.

"Sure, but I don't think we have any French bread for garlic bread. I could make some biscuits or corn bread . . . nah, corn bread just doesn't go with spaghetti, does it?"

"Can't we just put some slices of bread under the broiler that ave been sprinkled with butter and garlic salt?"

"We can do that. Salad?"

"Sure but I'll pass on the onions."

"Done. Anything else?"

"Wine?"

"Are you still taking pain killers?" she asked.

"Nope, I stopped. I take an occasional Tylenol but that's all."

"Then we'll celebrate with, say, a red?"

Greg gave her a thumbs up and she disappeared into the kitchen. He was looking forward to a home-cooked meal but felt guilty that he couldn't help. He picked up his laptop and continued surfing for the Ahren's Seep or Ahren's Creek in Pima or Yuma County, Arizona. He had lost count of how many pages of entries he had gone through but was getting frustrated at finding so many that, when opened, had nothing at all to do with either Ahren's Seep or Ahren's Creek.

Finally an idea came to him. First, surely Arizona had some kind of water governing board? Secondly, mightn't they have a file on the location of all the known tinajas through the state? He decided to confer with his cook before going further. He clomped into the kitchen on his crutches and found Jen boiling a pot of water for pasta and reading the label on a jar of spaghetti sauce.

"You don't have all the ingredients I need to make sauce from scratch, so you're going to have to settle for the jar kind supplemented with some mushrooms, olives and sausage. Can you live with that?"

Greg leaned against the door jamb and sighed, "If I must."

She smirked and waved a knife at him as she chopped up vegetables for the salad.

"Keep it up buddy, and you'll be washing the dishes."

"I was wondering, oh exalted guru of the internet, if the great State of Arizona has some bureaucratic agency for water that might have a record of all the known tinajas preferably in Yuma and Pima Counties. After all, I have nothing but time and could look to see if there's a tributary that is associated with said tinaja."

"There must be hundreds if not thousands of tinajas in the state, in fact I have a map of the tinajas on the BMGR," said Jen. If they could be narrowed down to Yuma and Pima Counties, it would help a lot, but that's still a daunting undertaking. And there's no guarantee Ahren's Seep or Ahren's Creek will show up. I have been searching water ways too but no harm in trying."

"Can you think of anything else I can try?"

"I think, with enough time, I could think of something else, but a search of the Arizona Department of Water Resources for tinajas isn't a bad idea even considering how time consuming it would be. You sure you want to give it a try?"

"Why not? It's either that or video games and soaps.

There's another thing to consider. If your robber is on the trail of the gold claim – which we agree he most likely is – he'll have to do the same things we've been doing but without the resources. If I was that robber and used to instant gratification, I'd probably just keep an eye on you and let you do the heavy lifting. If he crosses my trail, he won't be any wiser but if he sees your name, he might think he's on to something."

"I suppose that makes sense," said Jen, pausing what she was doing. "The guy didn't strike me as computer oriented so I'm not too worried about him tracking me on the net."

"I worry that he has friends who are."

"They'll have to hack in to what I'm doing and I have some pretty good malware, anti-virus and firewall protection. I'll know if someone tries."

"Good enough. How long until dinner?"

"Maybe twenty minutes. Enough time for you to get started on your search, so get after it!"

"Okay, okay. Sheesh!" He hobbled his way back to the couch, eased himself down and picked up his laptop. He started his search with the Arizona Department of Water Resources. Greg found the site superficial and not at all helpful for his search. He debated calling into the agency but wasn't up for the runaround he was sure to get. He thought maybe, like Jen's map, someone might have a map of the tinajas but it was going to be a long search mostly freelance through many pages of the internet.

He tried searches for anything close to "maps of tinajas in Pima and Yuma Counties" and found everything from swimming pool ads to free life vests to mosquito prevention! But he kept going, knowing that eventually the net would give up what he sought. There just *had* to be some kind of record of Ahren's Seep or Ahren's Creek tucked away in some musty map in one county or the other.

Jen interrupted his search by carrying in a plate mounded

with spaghetti and covered with a marinara sauce loaded with mushrooms, olives and slices of Italian sausage. Next came a plate with "garlic bread," another with salad, then she poured glasses of cabernet sauvignon.

Greg willingly set down his laptop on the end table and was eagerly eyeing the food on his plate. Jen sat down next to him with her own plate and said, "Dig in." He complied with a will and had nothing to say for several minutes. Finally, after dabbing the corners of his mouth with a napkin, he said, "Jen, this is just super, you must have learned to cook from an Italian."

She swallowed a bite of salad and said, "Actually, my mom taught me, and she's as French Canadian as they come."

"Well, you both know a thing or two about fixing spaghetti, thank you."

"You're welcome. How are you doing on your search?"

His face fell, "Not really too well. There are so many variations to run down in searching for a seep or even a creek. There are public agencies monitoring and governing water just in Pima and Yuma counties and none of them seem to want to give up their information willingly."

"Bureaucracies are like that; they bury the needed information under layers of bullshit, excuse the expression."

"My thoughts exactly. How do you keep sane doing this all the time? Don't get me wrong, I'm happy to be doing this but I can't imagine making a career out of it."

"Me either but right now it's paying the bills and I look at every search as a treasure hunt and I have to fight my way through the flotsam and jetsam to get to the prize I was looking for."

"Well, now you appear to have real pirates after the same thing you're after. That doesn't make it that much fun but I guess we just have to find a way to adapt and keep you safe."

"Yeah, I kind of like that idea," Jen said drily.

They finished their meal, Jen refused to let Greg help clean up. He got up, went to the bathroom, then leaned against the same door jamb as Jen went about cleaning up the kitchen. He watched her easy, graceful movements then asked, "Do you dance? You have the grace and movement of a dancer."

"I'm not much of a dancer but Susan and I both do a lot of tae kwan do sparring."

"Really? How long have you been doing that?"

"Since I was fifteen," she said, "I'm a third dan black belt."

"That means you can turn me every which way but loose, right?"

She smiled and wiped her hands on a dish towel as she finished up. Then she put down the towel, walked over to Greg and slipped her arms around his waist. "I may turn you every which way but loose but not in the way you're thinking," she said throatily. She tilted her face up to be kissed and Greg was more than happy to oblige – several times. She backed away a little so Greg could get his crutches working and he hobbled over and eased down in his usual spot on the couch.

Jen followed him over and sat down close beside him once he was settled, and his leg was propped up on the coffee table. She leaned over into him, pressing her breasts into his arm. She tilted his head toward her and lasciviously kissed him again until they both had to catch their breath.

"You're killing me here, Jen," Greg whispered through heavy breathing. "Believe me, there's nothing I'd rather do than sweep you up in my arms, carry you into the bedroom and ravish you. I've racked my brain searching for a position that would work and I'm coming up empty, my knee is just too painful to try *any* position."

"That's okay, baby, I just want to keep your motor running."

"Trust me, it's over revving." He leaned over and nuzzled her neck causing her to take in a sharp breath. "How's *your* motor?" he whispered as he nibbled her ear lobe. She moaned in response and pressed herself closer to him, if that was even possible.

Finally she broke away and reached for her wine glass on the coffee table. She took a deep draught then looked over at him. "There's a law in this state against molesting young women," she said in a soft voice, taking another sip of wine before continuing, "I wish you could break it."

Greg had to laugh at their situation and, in a moment, she joined him. "Just so you know, it's not my choice not to break that law."

"Well, I don't think it's very nice to get a girl all hot and bothered then leave her hanging," she said petulantly, a smile twitching at the corners of her mouth. "There ought to be a law about that too."

"I know there should and I admit I'm guilty as hell. Why don't we go to bed and I'll see if I can find some way to make it up to you?"

Her smile of triumph made Greg suspect she had orchestrated this from the beginning. Not that he was unhappy about it.

They undressed to the buff like an old married couple and slid into opposite sides of the bed. Greg had perfected his one-legged swing into bed by using his good leg against his right like a splint. He paused a moment on his back then rolled onto his left side, keeping his right knee against his left.

"There! That's about the range of my mobility in bed," he said, reaching to pull her closer. She snuggled up next to him front to front as close as she could get. She could feel his hardness against her belly even as her erect nipples brushed against the hair of his chest.

"Now how can I make this up to you?" he asked softly, his face in her hair and his right hand roving over her back. Jen was more than happy to show him but he was a slow learner; it took most of the night.

CHAPTER 15

Alfredo Menendez spent the next three weeks watching Jen's apartment, waiting for her to show up. He varied his routine some, though he was always there at 6 A.M. to check for her car and for lights on inside the apartment. He was always disappointed on both counts. He called in to Jimbo McVey every day and listened to him rant about Alfredo's inability to make something happen. Alfredo assured the lawyer that he was doing everything he could and eventually it would pay off. He would either catch the bitch herself at the apartment, and beat the rest of the story out of her or he would follow someone from the apartment to their hideout.

Greg and Jen were thriving on their forced sabbatical Certainly neither was bored with their research or with each other. Greg's knee was healing well. His surgeon had cleared him to put weight on his knee when standing and to even walk without the aid of the crutches for short distances. To Greg, that meant walking freely around the apartment, and he would have accompanied Jesse to the store but Jen vetoed *that* idea. "You've invested a month in healing, Greg, do you want to risk going all the way back to the beginning just so you can walk around a store a little early?"

Jesse chimed in, "She's right Greg. Better stay put until the doc gives you the okay."

It was not what Greg wanted to hear from his wingman but he recognized the wisdom in their words, *Just a couple more weeks.* That didn't make his case of cabin fever any less trying – especially when Jen announced that she was going grocery shopping with Jesse because Jesse didn't know a ripe avocado from a pickle.

*****

After nearly four weeks, Alfredo was near the end of his

rope, not only in his efforts on behalf of Jimbo McVey but for himself. He didn't know what else to do to find this bitch and Jimbo wasn't going to wait forever. He'd put the word out among his considerable associates but no one had seen her. He checked the Post Office: yes, she was still listed as the resident at that apartment. No, they wouldn't tell him if she had a forwarding address without a subpoena or a court order. As much as he hated calling attention to himself, Alfredo even checked with some of her close neighbors but no one seemed to know anything about her and only knew her to say hello in passing – at least that's what they were telling an Hispanic male with gang tats all up and down his arms and a few on his face.

It was as he was coming out of the supermarket near Jen's apartment that it occurred to him to watch the store for her. It was close by and it stood to reason she would continue to use the same store unless she had moved miles away. He had nothing to lose since watching her apartment was such a bust.

Alfredo caught a break almost right away. Two days later, he was half watching for Jen's car and half watching for her going into the store when there she was! She was with some military-looking dude who was probably her fucking boyfriend. Alfredo didn't try to follow them into the store but changed his position so he would see them come out and likely see which car they were using.

"I don't know why we had to come all the way over here, there are stores closer to home, you know," grumbled Jesse. "We could have stopped at any one of them."

"This store has the freshest produce around and I know how the store is laid out. That means we'll get in and out faster than in a store I'm not familiar with." Jesse grimaced but said nothing.

In Jen's mind, she and Jesse finished their shopping in record time. He was not an attentive shopper but drove the cart and guarded Jen's purse while she shopped. As they left the store with their bags of groceries, as had become her habit, Jen remembered to look around for anyone suspicious but failed to see Alberto in a hat and sunglasses hunkered down below the top rim of his steering wheel. Alberto was excited. *Finally!*

Alfredo watched them get into a gray late model Highlander and drive away. Neither of them appeared to be looking around for someone following but he stayed as far back as he dared without losing them. That meant he had to run a few red lights to stay up with them but luck was in his favor and no cops stopped him.

They turned east on Grant and drove the speed limit all the way to Houghton, where Jesse signaled then turned into an apartment complex. Alfredo sped up a little to keep them in sight and followed them into the complex and around to the rear where Jesse suddenly pulled in to an empty space. Half panicked, Alfredo had no place to go but forward and he cruised by Jesse's Highlander just as its occupants were walking up the sidewalk toward the door of one of the ground floor apartments. *Number 153.* Alberto was confident he would remember the apartment when the time came to pay it a visit. He parked in a section farther down the lane next to a white Miata where he could still see Jesse's Highlander and sort of the front of the apartment. He didn't dare get any closer since there weren't any other cars for cover.

Not many minutes went by before the man Alfredo mistakenly assumed was Jen's boyfriend emerged from the apartment and drove away. Alfredo weighed the circumstances against the odds. The parking lot was nearly empty since most everyone had gone to work but he had done no surveillance, and he didn't know if there was anyone else in the apartment. Now was a very good time to grab the bitch and pound some truth out of her. Anticipating that he might have to take her to McVey if Alfredo failed to get the truth from her, he backed into a spot directly in front of the sidewalk that led to apartment 153. He checked his piece one more time and that he had a roll of duct tape under his jacket and got out of the car and cautiously walked up to the front door. He stood near the door and listened for sounds of conversation or anything else from inside but heard nothing.

Taking a deep breath, Alfredo knocked confidently on the door, again listening for any sounds from within. There was silence for several seconds then he heard footsteps as someone came to the door. He knocked again, keeping his head below the level of the security lens in the door.

"Who is it?" came Jen's voice through the door. She looked at Greg who was sitting on the couch with his leg up, his Glock in his hand.

"UPS, I have a package that requires a signature."

Greg nodded to Jen to open the door then signaled her to get away from the door when it opened. When she turned back the dead bolt and began to open the door, Alfredo put his shoulder into it and drove it open, pushing Jen back and she dove away from the doorway. Her movement allowed Greg a clear shot at whomever was coming through the doorway.

Alfredo staggered a step into the apartment from the force of his shove against the door, his roll of duct tape falling to the floor from beneath his jacket. As he recovered, he already had his gun in his hand but before he could bring it to bear, a loud, authoritative man's voice said, "Freeze. Drop the gun or die."

Alberto froze, buying himself a second or two to assess his situation. He saw Jen had fallen back away from the line of fire and was too far away to grab as a hostage. That left him with a man pointing a gun at Alfredo's center mass and him with his gun at his side. Alfredo had been figuring odds since he was a young scam artist and he rated his chances as poor to zero to get his gun up before the man put a bullet or three in him. He dropped the gun at his feet.

"Kick the gun over toward her," the man commanded, nodding toward Jen, his Glock never wavering. Alberto kicked the gun almost to Jen's feet, and she picked it up and aimed it at him. His odds of escaping had just dropped to zero.

"Hey man, I wasn't going to hurt nobody . . ."

"Shut up!" Alfredo shut up. Even with a bandaged knee,

this dude looked like someone who would shoot first and ask questions later and Alfredo wasn't about to piss him off. "Close the door and assume the position," the man ordered.

The door was only standing open a few inches and Alfredo knew that he would feel a bullet entering his back, possibly even his spine, before he could get through the doorway. He pushed the door shut.

"Assume the position against the door, arms up high and your chest against the door."

Feeling a little ridiculous, Alfredo complied. The position was uncomfortable and left him no room to react to an opportunity.

"Jen, get his roll of duct tape and tape his arms behind his back. Be sure to stay out of my line of fire."

It took Jen a minute to get the hang of tearing the duct tape in half when she wanted a new piece but soon she was wrapping the tape around Alfredo's wrists and forearms up to his elbows like a veteran. When she decided she was done, Alfredo was taped solidly from wrist to elbow with no give and not much comfort.

"Good. Now sit him down on the love seat and do the same thing to his ankles halfway up his calves. She complied and when she was through, Alfredo had no hope of going anywhere.

"Now search him. Take everything he's got on him and put it on the coffee table. Don't hesitate to search his crotch and don't be shy about searching thoroughly."

When she finished, there was little piled up on the table Twenty dollars in ones and fives, a few coins, a key, copies of the Cactus Wren Claim papers and a switchblade knife Jen had extracted from his boot. That had precipitated the removal of his boots and a second look at his socks. There was no wallet or any identification found anywhere.

"I guess we can dispense with questions about who you are and why you're here," said the man. "On second thought, maybe we don't know what you're doing here. Care to enlighten us?"

Alfredo's mind had been going at top speed trying to come

up with a believable lie but since these people knew who he was and what he was involved in, there was little use in denying it. He felt no loyalty to Jimbo McVey and would give him up for no reason at all – as long as it didn't get back to the big man.

"I don't know how to convince you we have no gold," the man with the gun said. The gold listed on that receipt you stole from Jen was turned over to the state over a hundred years ago. All we have are the same papers you saw – nothing more."

"What about the gold claim itself? Do you know where it is?" Alfredo blurted.

Jen interjected, "No! We have no more of an idea where the claim is than you do. Why can't you believe us?"

Alfredo felt he was fighting a losing battle but he persisted,

"Then why were you carrying those papers around with you?" he demanded, jutting his chin at the claim papers on the table.

"I give up!" said Greg in disgust. "This jerk will never believe us, I say we take him out into the desert and shoot him."

That's not far off from what's going to happen to me if I don't find that claim.

"My boss would not like that and he knows who I'm dealing with. He would come after you and he is a very powerful man."

"So we should just dust you off, pat you on the shoulder and let you go? I don't think so, you've pushed us way too far. At the very least you're going back to jail. I don't know how you managed to get out last time."

"Like I say, my boss is a very powerful man. A well-known lawyer and someone not accustomed to not getting his way."

"And just who is this boss of yours? If he's a lawyer and behind your robberies of Jen, he'll be disbarred and proseccuted."

"His name is Jimbo McVey. If you do not know him you'd better ask. He has been around a long time and knows everyone in Pima County," Alfredo boasted. "He is very well-connected and has people working for him who are very dangerous."

"To hell with this!" Greg exclaimed. Let's call the police

111

and get this piece of shit out of here. All I can tell you is that if you ever get out of jail, and come around here again, I won't hesitate to blow you away and you'd better believe I'll do it."

Alfredo believed him. Now he had to go back to jail and this time, with another *armed* robbery charge facing him, even Jimbo McVey wouldn't be able to get him out of this.

"One last thing," said Jen, rising from the couch. She walked over to where Alfredo was sitting and, with no warning, laid a roundhouse kick alongside his head that left him stunned and unable to talk or move.

"That's for backhanding me last time, you piece of shit. If you *ever* try to touch me again, it'll be the last thing you ever do."

CHAPTER 16

After the last Tucson PD officer had left, having completed their usual thorough investigation, Greg thought to look up the name of Jimbo McVey. Alfredo had not been lying, McVey was well-represented on the internet and was clearly a high-powered, high-priced defense attorney. There was little on the web suggesting that McVey was crooked but Greg had a good friend, Major Woodrow Jamison, with the Air Force MPs who probably had heard of McVey.

"Jimbo McVey? Oh sure, he's well known in criminal defense circles as the go to guy in tough cases. Why?"

"One of his henchmen, a guy named Alfredo Menendez, has been harassing a friend of mine – has robbed her three times – and bragged that he works for McVey and whatever McVey wants, McVey gets."

"Robbed her? *Three* times? Why isn't the bastard in jail?"

"He is – again – after we caught him breaking into my apartment, with a gun. First time, he was fencing for a smash and grab artist, the second time my friend identified him from a photo display and this last time, we caught him in the act. McVey got him out of jail on the second robbery."

"What's his problem?"

"He believes she has some gold, and he wants it."

"I won't even ask about the gold angle."

"Oh, I found some papers a while back and among them was a receipt from a bank for forty-two ounces of gold. The receipt was dated in 1889. The gold was never claimed and wound up going to the state under the escheatment laws. This bozo believes that my friend has it and is bound and determined to get it for none other than Jimbo McVey."

"McVey and I don't run in the same circles, if you know what I mean, but I have a buddy with Tucson PD's Organized Crime Unit who probably knows him a lot better than me. His name is Salazar, Sergeant Bud Salazar, I have his card here somewhere." Greg could hear his friend shuffling around his desk. He finally found the card and read off the phone number.

"Give him a call, if he doesn't know about McVey, I'll be surprised; but if he doesn't, he'll hook you up with someone who does."

Greg got lucky and caught Sergeant Salazar just leaving the office. He quickly explained the reason for the call and that he had been referred by his friend, Major Jamison.

"How's ol' Woodrow doing?" asked Sergeant Salazar.

"He's doing well. I heard he's on the early promotion list to lieutenant colonel."

"I'm happy for him, he deserves it but for selfish reasons, I'm sorry to hear that."

"Why's that?"

"Woody's great to work with when we have a case that overlaps civilian and military. I'll be sad to see him go, as I assume he will, to another post with more responsibility."

"Yeah, that's usually the way it works."

"Jimbo McVey, huh? Your friend owe him money?"

"Nope." Greg explained the circumstances.

"I've heard rumors about McVey for the past ten years, that he's connected to the mob, that he loan sharks, deals in prostitution and gambling and has even been said to be involved in a killing or two. He's on our radar but we've never even been close to making a case on him. I don't suppose your bad guy, what was his name? Alfredo Menendez, would roll on him would he?"

"I have no idea," said Greg, "he didn't hesitate to name him so maybe he isn't as tight with him as he'd like us to believe."

"Maybe I'll send someone over to chat with Menendez at the

jail. Would you or your friend mind if we negotiated away some – not all, mind you – of the charges against him to induce him to work for us on McVey?"

Greg chuckled. "I don't have a problem with that as long as he sees the inside of a prison for a while and I don't think my friend would mind either. She got her pound of flesh from him before the police took Menendez away this last time. You'll understand if you see his mug photo after arrest; the whole left side of his face is black and blue."

"What did she do, hit him with a two by four?"

"No, just a very angry right foot."

"Good for her! Getting back to McVey, stay as far away from him and his men as you can. Like I said, there's talk that he was involved in a murder or two and he has some people working for him who are capable of anything."

"Well, thank you Sergeant, for taking the time to talk with me, rest assured we'll heed your advice." After hanging up, Greg relayed what he had learned to Jen. "Somehow, I don't think we've seen the end of this just because Menendez is back in jail. We need to remain very vigilant. By the way, nice job dodging out of the way when Menendez forced his way in. Oh, and thank you for not breaking his nose, it's very expensive to get blood cleaned out of upholstery. I think the half face shiner is more telling anyway."

Jen giggled as she walked from the kitchen entrance to where Greg was sitting on the couch. She sat down next to him, leaned over and gave him a passionate kiss. "An angry foot,' huh?"

Just then they heard a key in the front door lock and Jesse and Susan walked in. Jesse stopped in his tracks and Susan ran into him as Jen pulled away from Greg. "Hell's fire, I guess we should start knockin' since I don't live here anymore, huh?"

"Yeah," said Greg, tongue in cheek, "and turn in your keys too! You guys missed all the fun! We caught Jen's robber, *again,* and the cops just hauled him off to jail."

"Is this guy desperate or just crazy?" asked Susan.

"I suspect a little bit of both," said Jen and went on to explain the details of their latest contact with Alfredo Menendez. Greg took over and related what he had learned from Sergeant Salazar. That sobered everyone and once again they discussed security issues.

"How the hell do you defend against someone who can strike anywhere at any time?" asked Jesse. "Hell, you can't even go to a local store and feel safe."

"I guess we get used to being hyper-vigilant all of the time," Susan commented with a shrug. "Sounds like Jesse's signals came in handy after all."

"Well," said Jesse with a nod, "not to change the subject but to change the subject, yours truly will be gone prospecting this weekend. I saw a guy over at Susan's apartment loading mining gear into pickup and asked him about it. Seems he's been prospecting in the Dome Rock Mountains near Quartzsite for years and claims to have been doing pretty well. We hit it off and he invited me to go along if I was willing to work. I told him I was. We'll camp out overnight and be back on Sunday. Hopefully I'll be rich enough by then that we can turn our backs on the Cactus Wren claim."

"Here here!" everyone chorused.

Greg said, "I'm still chasing that damned tinaja or creek but I finally ordered and received some old maps of the area around the Growler Mountains where I crashed. I haven't gone over them yet but hope springs eternal. I had hoped that by the time I was back to a hundred percent, we could be traipsing around the outback in search of our landmarks but I may be a little premature."

"Everyone knows that that whole area is either military reservation or wildlife conservation land, right? Prospecting is prohibited," said Jen.

"Then I reckon we'll have to trespass," said Jesse fiercely, "'cause I ain't givin' up that damned easy, especially after all that has happened to you!"

"We're all in agreement on that, honey," said Susan as she

walked up beside him, brushed her hand over his shoulders and rubbed his back.

"Oh, I know," Jesse conceded, "it just pisses me off when other people impose themselves on me or mine and I can't do anything about it."

"None of us are going to risk going to Leavenworth, either," said Greg firmly. "I don't think there's a greedy bone in any of our bodies so we should look at this in the perspective of an adventure of sorts, not as a life or death project."

Everyone nodded and Jesse looked a little sheepish.

"Susan," asked Jen, "have you had a chance to research gold buyers?"

Susan rolled her eyes. "Oh brother what a tangle that was! There are more gold buyers out there than I ever dreamed and over half of them will cheat you at the first blush. I finally called my bank and, on the QT, got the names of three reputable gold buyers here in Tucson from the bank's president. Anytime we have something to sell, I know where to take it. I also learned that Brinks has precious metals storage and will pick it up and deliver it too. They charge a percentage fee, somewhere around three quarters of a percent."

"At last! Something to cross off our list," Jen exclaimed with a smile.

"You know, we came over here to see if you two wanted to go to the O-Club for dinner. Greg, are you up for that?"

"Sure, as long as I'm careful and still use the crutches in wide open spaces, I'm good to go. These last two weeks are going to take forever. I'm so looking forward to getting rid of these sticks."

"You remember that when you're suffering through the PT that is sure to come. Your leg will need a lot of strengthening before it's ready to hike 'them thar hills'," said Susan.

"I'll remember every second of this . . . until I'm back in the cockpit of an A-10. Then it will seem like a bad memory with some bright spots in it," said Greg as he leaned over and kissed Jen on the cheek.

The next morning at 0630, Jesse emerged from Susan's apartment yawning and stretching to meet his prospecting mentor, Dave Gainey. They loaded Jesse's gear in Gainey's well-used Isuzu Trooper then drove over to the Black Bear Diner for an early breakfast. It would be a three and a half hour drive or more to Quartzsite then another forty-five minutes into Dave's claim in the Dome Rock Mountains south and west of town.

When they got settled in a booth and placed their orders, Dave took a sip of his coffee and looked at Jesse. "So you don't know anything about prospecting?"

"Nary a thing. I'm pretty good at reading a topo map, bombing the shit out of a target and I know one end of a pick from the other but that's about it."

Gainey laughed. He was a tall, slender, slightly stooped man in his sixties with graying hair and a ready smile. A retired high school math teacher and coach, he had admitted to Jesse that he had begun prospecting after he retired because he was bored, then the gold bug had bit him. He wasn't looking to get rich prospecting on the small scale that he was, but he was surprised at how well he had been doing, and how good his physical condition was because of it.

"Mining a placer claim isn't like blasting away rock and finding veins of gold in quartz. And it isn't rocket science. This is strong back, weak mind employment at my level, but when you find those little gold particles, it's all worth the work, at least to me.

"Unless you have the technical resources to really analyze a geologic area, which I certainly don't, you search for gold in places where gold has been found before. In my case, looking in dried up streambeds in such an area that has yielded a fair amount of gold before is the best way to find gold but, like I said, I'm not going to get rich.

"Ground water leaches gold particles from a deposit and

those particles get washed down streambeds and settle in slow-moving water. Gold is heavy than most anything else and tends to settle out faster than most other sediments so you look in pockets downstream from some kind of obstacle like a large rock formation or a curve in the stream bank where there is lee protection from the current.

"That's when the strong back comes into play since you need to separate the finer sediment from the larger stuff then keep winnowing down the waste until the only things left are gold particles and fine sand. You dig sediment out of the streambed, vacuum gravel and sand from lee areas and anywhere else gold is likely to settle.

"The claim I'm working now is an old wash, not very wide, that apparently has been ignored by other prospectors. At least I haven't found tailings and holes in or around it and I have been finding gold. Tailings are piles of debris left over from the winnowing process."

Just then their breakfasts arrived and Gainey was content to mostly table the prospecting discussion in favor of chowing down. "When we get to the claim, we'll unload my equipment, set up camp and get to work."

CHAPTER 17

Jesse insisted on paying for breakfast and the two men were on their way, driving I-10 from Tucson to Quartzsite. The old Trooper shook dust all over the interior and, at seventy miles an hour, seemed to be wheezing its last breath but kept going.

"For most of today, we'll both be digging and vacuuming out gravel and sand from the wash then filtering what we dig through screens that fit over the top of five-gallon buckets. We'll look through what didn't pass through the screens for anything interesting – like nuggets – then discard what's left. When we get far enough ahead in that process, you'll keep screening while I fire up the dry washer and start winnowing down the buckets of sand and gravel into just sand and, hopefully, gold. The final step, other than collecting the gold, is to pan the gold away from the sand. We have enough gas for the generator and water to pan most of what we dig."

"Electricity?" asked Jesse.

"Yeah. I use an electric panner powered by a small generator. It's more reliable than my eyes at separating the gold from the loose sand. I know this is a thumbnail sketch of the process, it'll make more sense when you see it in action."

After they turned off I-10 at Quartzsite, Gainey drove them halfway through the sleepy town until he signaled a turn south onto Highway 95.

"I've heard of Quartzsite but I've never been here. It looks kind of abandoned. I thought it was a pretty busy place."

"Give it another month or two and it'll be overrun with snowbirds. At its peak," said Gainey, "the place is crowded with rock hounds, tourists and people looking for bargains or unique things in the stalls that crowd both sides of the freeway. There isn't much you can't find here from books to recreational vehicles.

There's a big gem and mineral show in February each year and a giant RV show in January. This becomes a very popular place."

"So we're just a little early being here in November?"

"Pretty much, which suits me fine. Just south of town is what is known as a Long Term Visitor's Area administered by the Bureau of Land Management. Here, for an annual fee of $180 you can camp for seven months in the winter. It's very popular and, at the season's peak, it almost seems you can walk across the desert on the roofs of all the RVs. My claim isn't that far from the LTVA so I worry about people jumping my claim when I'm not around."

"Has that happened, claim jumpers, that is?"

"Not that I know of but I've only been working this claim for about six months," said Gainey with a shrug.

"What could you do if you caught someone? Are you armed?"

"No, I don't carry a gun, that usually leads to unfortunate consequences and I'm sure as hell not going to shoot someone who is trespassing on a piece of federal land."

"But they might be stealing your gold!" Jesse pointed out.

"Oh, I wouldn't just throw my hands up and walk away. I'd contact BLM and the local ranger and, hopefully, get them thrown out if not arrested. I'm just not going to take the law into my own hands."

"You're awfully understanding about it," Jesse observed.

"When you're my age, you develop a different perspective."

Just then, Gainey made a right turn off Highway 95 onto a rough, unmaintained dirt road that led up into the Dome Rock Mountains. The desert had changed from the Sonora to the Mojave and plant life was much scarcer. Creosote bushes dominated the sere landscape along with occasional Mesquite and Ironwood trees. Even the cacti, famous in Sonora Desert scenes, was mainly AWOL.

"Almost there," he grunted just as they ran over a particularly obnoxious rock. He shifted into four low and started to crawl up a steep trail that could hardly be called a road. Rock outcroppings seemed to oppose the Trooper's progress but it just slowly crawled over all the opposition. Finally they reached a fairly wide, seemingly flat section of wash and Gainey slowed to a stop behind a beat up old faded green International pickup. The tailgate was down and there were ten five-gallon-buckets of sand/small gravel in the bed ahead of a loose pile of mining equipment.

Two men appeared walking toward the pickup from a slight bend in the wash upstream of the pickup. They were dressed nearly alike in work boots, jeans and long-sleeved flannel shirts. One was taller and heavier than the other but both had scraggly beards and greasy hair under their ballcaps. Each man carried two more buckets of matrix.

Jesse immediately didn't like their looks and reached into the back seat, fumbled around in his backpack until he withdrew his Glock.

"What's that for?" Gainey asked, nodding at the handgun.

"Insurance."

Gainey got out of the Trooper and stepped forward to greet the two men. "Mornin' boys. How're you doing today?" Jesse got out too but stayed behind the door of the Trooper, his hand holding the gun out of sight.

"Mornin'," mumbled the taller of the two men. They stopped about forty feet in front of Gainey and set down their buckets.

"What do you want?" the bigger man asked brusquely.

"Well," Gainey drawled, "I'm wonderin' what you're doing on my claim."

"This ain't your claim, you're mistaken," snarled the bigger man.

"That's one of the corner posts up there at the top of the wash," Gainey said, nodding up the hill.

Neither man bothered to look up in the direction Gainey indicated, but continued to stare at Gainey, barely aware of Jesse. "It *is* my claim and I'm afraid I'm going to have to confiscate what you have in the buckets."

The big man took a couple more steps, without his buckets and folded his arms across his chest. "You ain't confiscatin' nothin'."

"That matrix belongs to me, it came off my claim," Gainey insisted.

"Come and get it," challenged the big man, taking another step toward Gainey, drawing a large hunting knife from his belt.

Jesse stepped from around the Trooper's door and, holding the Glock down by his leg, joined Gainey at the front of the Trooper.

"Reckon y'all better put that away before someone gets hurt."

The man looked at Jesse then down at the Glock.

"Fine. You can have the sand; we're leavin'"

As the two men walked toward the International, Jesse said, "That includes what's in y'all's pickup too."

"Fuck that!" exclaimed the smaller man, "We worked our asses off for that!"

"But you did it on someone else's claim, and got caught," said a frozen-faced Jesse. "Now unload them buckets out of your pickup, now!"

"That's not right," whined the smaller man, "those buckets are ours, we paid five dollars apiece for them."

"And you just forfeited them by filling them with stolen matrix from another man's claim," said Jesse.

"Asshole," the small man muttered as he and his partner walked the rest of the way to the pickup.

"Oh," added Jesse, "If you try to take off without unloading the buckets, I'll flatten both your front tires and perforate your radiator."

"Fucking asshole," muttered the smaller man as he and his partner walked to the rear of the pickup and unloaded the buckets right in front of the Trooper. After unloading the buckets and closing the tailgate, both men got in the pickup, and Gainey and

Jesse watched them turn around and drive off, their middle fingers waving out of both side windows.

"Well, I'm glad neither of them had a gun," said Gainey.

"I'd bet they're both ex-cons and that's the only reason they didn't," Jesse opined. When they couldn't hear the exhaust leak on the International any longer, both men relaxed and looked around them.

"Honey, we're home," Gainey quipped as he turned back toward his vehicle.

Jesse took a longer look around him. Judging by the plant growth, it did not appear that water had flowed in this wash for a long time but when it had, it was formidable. Large tree trunks were tangled together at a downstream bend in the wash and recliner-chair-sized boulders littered what would have been rapids had there been water. Jesse could see what looked like a tent site below an Ironwood tree in the sand upstream from the Trooper and there was a fire ring nearby

"Okay, hopefully we've seen the last of those two," said Gainey. "Why don't we unload the gear? If you're comfortable setting up the tent and the campsite, I'll see to the mining gear." It was a nice way to ask if Jesse was capable of setting up the camp.

Jesse nodded, put the Glock back in his backpack and went to work. He first unloaded the two-man tent and carried it to the tent site. "Dave, I'm a little turned around here. Where does the prevailing wind come from? I don't reckon we want the door of the tent facing that way." Gainey nodded approvingly and pointed downstream. Jesse laid the tent out with the door facing upstream. He found it almost impossible to drive tent stakes into the bed of the wash and wound up using heavy rocks to anchor the corners. He then raised the tent and put their clothes, sleeping bags and pads inside.

Next came a long folding table he set up next to the tent, and placed the two-burner stove and the lantern on it. He hoisted the grub box out of the back of the Trooper and placed it under the table along with two ice chests, four five-gallon jugs of water and a five-gallon container of gasoline. Finished with what he could see of the camping gear, Jesse started gathering firewood and stacking it near the fire ring.

"Can I help you with the equipment?" he asked Gainey as Jesse dropped the last load of firewood near the fire ring.

"Nah, just about got it. You all set?"

"Yep. What's next?"

"We're going to have to hump the equipment upstream about a hundred yards to the mouth of the wash. Just watch your footing, don't want you to break an ankle on the rocks." He paused, looking off upstream in the distance.

"But first, let's go see where our friends were digging," said Gainey, backtracking in the direction the two trespassers had come. Sure enough, they had been digging in Gainey's wash.

As they walked back down to camp, Gainey said, "On second thought, let's pan what our friends left us first; that should take at least today. If we do this right, you might not have to do any digging or burro work at all."

"Burro work?" asked Jesse.

"Lugging full five-gallon buckets of screened material down the wash we're mining to the bottom so we can run it through the dry washer."

"I suspect that's going to be the best offer I get all day," Jesse observed.

"I think you're right," said Gainey with a laugh.

They set up a plastic tub, and emptied one of the five-gallon jugs of water into it. Then, as Jesse started hauling the buckets of matrix closer, Gainey set up the spiral wheel concentrator and the generator. The concentrator was an awkward-looking affair. Set up on a sturdy tripod over the tub the spiral wheel itself looked much like a conventional gold pan with a spiral ridge embossed around the bottom. It was set up on an angle and a hose run from low pressure jets to a pump and then into the tub. The electric motor that turned the spiral wheel and drove the water pump was plugged into the generator.

When energized, the contraption started to spin slowly on an angle and water began dribbling down from the jets onto the spiral wheel with one more water line flushing out the unwanted debris at the bottom. Once again, the idea was that the gold, being heavier, would remain in the spirals while the ejecta was washed away. The gold would eventually spiral into the center and into a catch bottle.

It was a slow process feeding matrix into the lower lip of the spiral pan and letting the water wash away the debris as it rose up the spiral guides. Gainey agreed that it was slow but faster and more reliable than hand panning.

They took a break at about 3:30 in the afternoon and had a long drink of water and a snack. Gainey retrieved the gold catch bottle and, sure enough, Jesse could see little particles of gold shining back at him.

They quit for the day at about six that evening and Gainey transferred the gold they had recovered into a small water-filled vial about three eighths of an inch in diameter and two inches long. He told Jesse that when full, the vial weighed close to an ounce.

By lantern light, they cooked a light dinner and turned in early.

CHAPTER 18

It took Dave and Jesse until 2 PM the next day to finish all the buckets of matrix. They had started at 6:30 AM and had not stopped even for lunch, only a water break. They had had to dig the silt out of the bottom of the tub every hour to make room for the fresh matrix. Jesse was more than tired of shoveling matrix into the concentrator and would almost have welcomed some real shoveling or burro work for a change of pace.

Finally Dave called a halt and announced that they should break camp and head back to Tucson since Susan was expecting Jesse that evening. They discussed the parts of the mining process Jesse had missed and, from the sound of it, he figured he didn't miss anything important.

When they returned to Tucson, Dave put the Trooper in park in the apartment parking lot and looked at Jesse.

"I'm going back out next weekend," said Dave, "you're welcome to come along if you want."

"I can't," Jesse replied, "I have the duty at the air base and I am scheduled to fly a mission as well."

"Well, we can't let you get out of practicing flying that A-10 around, can we? Let's just say you're welcome anytime you can break free, okay?"

"How about the weekend after? I don't think Susan or I have anything planned and I think she could handle feeding the matrix into the concentrator if you have no objection. I think she'd like the experience."

"Okay by me but you'll have to bring your own tent, mine isn't big enough for three."

"Great! I'm looking forward to it."

"Oh, and Jesse? This belongs to you," said Dave as he

handed Jesse a glass vial about half full of gold particles in water. I figure that's about half of what we got this weekend and I'm not one to hog all the profits. I figure there's maybe seven hundred dollars worth of gold there assuming it's pure or nearly so."

"Hell's fire! Thanks Dave, but I didn't expect to get paid. No, this belongs to you, you're the one who found it. Remember? I just came out to see how it's done and you have been an excellent teacher."

"No, Jesse, you keep it. Besides, you earned it, had you not been there, I'd have recovered nothing but a passel of trouble from those two guys."

"Think they'll come back?"

"Your guess is as good as mine. Hopefully they hadn't processed any of the matrix and didn't know how rich it was."

"So the stuff we processed would be considered rich?"

"Jesse, they measure commercial gold yield by the *gram* per metric ton. Anything over eight grams per ton is exceptional. A Troy ounce weighs a little over 31.1 grams and we probably harvested an ounce to an ounce and a quarter out of, what? Fourteen buckets of matrix? Yeah, that would be considered pretty rich."

"I'll be damned," said Jesse, flabbergasted. "Sounds like you found yourself a gold strike."

"Yeah, maybe, though it could peter out at any time and often does. Yeah, it might be a good strike assuming those guys don't come back."

"Might be time to buy that gun we were talking about, Dave."

"I wish you were wrong but I'm afraid you're right. I don't know anything about guns, could you advise me?"

"Better yet, let's get y'all enrolled in a concealed carry safety course that'll teach you the basics. A friend of mine just went through one and learned the basics of handling a weapon and got to fire one she bought on an approved range. That's better than shooting at cans in the desert."

"Can you help me pick something out?"

"Sure. We can go shopping any evening this coming week if you want. In the meantime, I'd better get my gear and head out before my sweetie comes looking for me."

They said their goodbyes and Jesse walked into Susan's apartment. "Susie darlin', are y'all home?"

"I'm in the kitchen," she called.

He walked into the kitchen where Susan had just started warming up dinner.

She stopped what she was doing to give Jesse a quick kiss and a hug then said, "You don't look any worse for wear, how did it go?"

"Much better than I had a right to expect. Ol' Dave's a straight shooter." He went on to tell her about their run in with the trespassers and how he had managed to avoid the burro work. Then he showed her the gold vial. "He gave me this for helping him today."

"That doesn't seem like very much," she offered.

"Sweetie, that's about seven hundred dollars worth of gold."

"You're kidding!"

"No ma'a-m. "Ol' Dave figures there's the better part of half an ounce here and gold is going for between $1700-$1800 an ounce.

"So you're underestimating its value?"

"Maybe. Purity hasn't been established yet. Purty, ain't it?"

"And valuable. Is this what the gold will look like if we find the Cactus Wren claim?"

"I'm guessing so, Dave says it could be in nugget form, dust or particles like this. I don't care, as long as it's gold."

"Let's go show Jen and Greg!" Susan exclaimed on impulse.

"Why don't we eat first then go? I mean, you have stuff on the stove and everything."

"Oh . . . yeah. Okay, then we'll show them!"

When Susan showed Jen the vial, Jen said, "It's beautiful, so that's what all the fuss is about. Um, how do we tell it's not fool's gold?"

"I asked Dave that," said Jesse. "Fool's gold is crystalline and the edges are sharp like crystals whereas gold has rounded edges and is more malleable. Fool's gold shines in direct light but fades in shadow; gold has a sheen even in low light. It's gold alright."

"So that's what we're after. Good going, Jesse. Are you going to go back out with Dave or did you learn what you needed to know?" asked Greg after examining the water-filled vial.

"Oh, I'm definitely going back out with Dave; matter of fact, I thought I'd see if Susan wanted to go with me. She could easily run the concentrator while Dave and I dug, vacuumed and screened. We'd be out there overnight. What do you think, Susan?"

"I'd *love* it!" she exclaimed. "Lately I've been feeling like haven't been carrying my share. It sounds like fun being out in the desert overnight. I've always wanted to camp in the desert, but never had anyone to take me who knew what they were doing."

Jesse laughed. "Well, thanks to Dave, you do now."

"How are you two doing on finding Ahren's Seep? Susan asked Jen.

"We're both just plugging away full time but that's going to change pretty soon. Greg has his final appointment with the surgeon next week and that will determine when he can go back to work."

"Greg, do you have an appointment with the flight surgeon yet?" asked Jesse.

"No. I thought I should get clearance from my surgeon before I set that up. I'm hoping it's just a rubber stamp of the surgeon's release."

Jesse shrugged. "Having never broke a knee cap, I don't reckon I have much experience to share."

"Greg, you've been off that leg more or less for six weeks, the doctor – whomever he is – is going to order several weeks of physical therapy before you're fully released," said Susan.

Greg sighed. "Yeah, I guess. I was hoping everyone would

forget about that."

"Not likely," said Jesse, "they'll want you in tip top shape before letting you back in a cockpit."

"Well, we have one more week to find our claim. I know what I have to do, does everyone else?"

"Going out with Dave again will have to skip a weekend, I have the duty and I'm scheduled for a mission this coming weekend," said Jesse.

"I guess I have the same assignment as Greg but from a different angle but I think my plate is full," said Jen.

"Gee, Jesse, looks like you'll have to take Susan shopping for what she needs to camp in the desert. Be sure to itemize them in our ledger and the gold too," said Greg.

"You're a hard taskmaster, Greg Miller, but I'll do it," said Jesse with a grin. "That reminds me, I'm goin' to take Dave out gun shopping one evening this week. Is anyone else in the market?"

"I'll stick with my Sig," said Susan. "It's loud but it fits my hand well and I like the fact it's a 9mm."

Jen had just finished her concealed carry training course and was carrying her Smith and Wesson everywhere. "I like my little Smith and Wesson," she said, "it's loud too but I like the fit and I'm comfortable with it."

Neither man would be parted from his Glock 22 .40 caliber.

"It's been quiet since Jen's assailant was arrested and kept in jail," said Greg, "but we have to expect further action since he even said he was working for Jimbo McVey. McVey doesn't sound like the type willing to give up easily. Since his number one stooge is in the slammer, he'll have to send someone else and the type he'll send will probably up the ante so we have to be careful."

*****

Jimbo McVey was tired and short-tempered. He had had a bad day and it had started with that idiot Alfredo Menendez. McVey had gone to the jail to talk with him and find out why he was back *in* jail. Alfredo was apologetic to the point of pleading that he had had no chance when he made his move against the bitch and her surprise boyfriend.

"I did everything right, followed her to the apartment and waited until the man left. I pretended I had a package that needed a signature and she opened the door just like she should. How was I to know there was another dude in there with a gun? He made me drop my piece and then they taped me up like a mummy with my own tape!"

"What happened to your face? Did the cops beat you up?" By now, the left side of his face was swollen almost beyond recognition. His eye was swollen completely shut and a deep blue green had set in around the eye and cheekbone.

"No. The bitch kicked me in the face after I was taped up, said if I ever touched her again she'd kill me. She's crazy! If I ever see her again and I have my blade, we'll see who kills who."

"What did they tell you about the gold?"

"They said there wasn't no gold, that the state got it a long time ago and that's all they knew."

"Yeah yeah, I know all that. What about the mine? The gold mine?"

"They didn't know nothing about it or where it was. Honest Mr. McVey, I did everything right, I was just unlucky."

"Well, your luck has changed for the better, you're in here instead of outside where I could get my hands on you."

After his meeting with Alfredo, McVey had to defend his motion to suppress in a big drug case and the judge ruled against him. The hearing had taken all morning and into the afternoon. He had been depending on that motion to suppress the evidence and now he would have to resort to other means to win the case.

"Send for Lester Cortez," Jimbo McVey ordered tersely

through his intercom to his receptionist. "Tell him I have a job for him."

Anyone who was anyone in the criminal scene in Tucson knew that Lester Cortez was an independent contract fixer for anyone with the money to pay his high fees. He was smart, effective and deadly when necessary. He had never failed to accomplish the goal for which he was hired. Greg Miller was more correct than he knew when he predicted what kind of thug Jimbo McVey would send against them.

"Mr. McVey, Mr. Cortez is here to see you."

"Send him in."

His receptionist tapped on his office door then opened it for Lester Cortez. He was impressive. Six feet tall and built like a middle linebacker with no neck and a waistline any woman would envy. He was darkly tanned with military short dark hair and the coldest dark eyes McVey had ever seen. Former Special Forces, Cortez believed in keeping himself in shape and honing his martial arts and firearms skills frequently.

McVey nodded to one of the chairs on the other side of his enormous desk and Cortez took a seat. Instead of speaking, McVey tossed a sheaf of papers in front of Cortez. Cortez picked them up and started reading the letter and the other papers Greg Miller had found less than two months ago.

When Cortez finished, he looked at McVey; his eyes never left the attorney's face. It was unsettling, to say the least. "Now you know as much as anyone, except the forty-two ounces of gold were confiscated by the state many years ago. My question is the location of the claim. It may have already been worked, it may not be accessible or it might be waiting for someone to find it again. I want to know what the finders of these papers know about the location of the mine, and I want to know when they find it and where it is."

He handed him another sheet of paper. On it were the names and locations of the players as McVey knew them. It did not include the names of Susan Liu or Jesse Grimes though Grimes was described. Included were the known cars used by the group. No occupations or places of employment were listed because Alfredo had failed to procure them.

"The man at the apartment on Houghton is armed, I have no corresponding information on the others. One last thing," said McVey as Cortez started to get up, "The man I had working on this before you was all brawn and no brains and got nothing of the information I require. I don't want these people molested in any way. I don't even want them to know that you exist. Find out what I want to know about them and then I'll decide what actions to take. Clear?"

Cortez nodded as he stood up. He paused, then reached down, gathered up the papers and put them in an inside coat pocket. He turned and walked out of the office; he had not uttered one word.

CHAPTER 19

The next morning, after breakfast, Greg sat down with the same old pile of maps he had been poring over for days. He had ordered a shotgun variety of maps of the Growler Mountains, Arizona, from the USGS and had received a shotgun variety of maps! He noticed one he hadn't examined, an 1887 map of the Territory of Arizona, and spread the two feet by three feet page across the coffee table. He quickly found the Growler Mountains and began examining them through a magnifying glass.

At first his brain couldn't grasp what his eyes were telling it. Ahren's Seep was printed neatly on the map nearly at the base of a pass through the Growlers! That pass through the Growler Mountains could only be what was now called Charlie Bell Pass. It was only a few peaks south of where Greg's A-10 had crashed.

"Jen? Could you come in here for a minute?" Greg called.

"I'll be right there."

Moments later she walked into the living room. Her reading glasses had slid down on her nose and, to Greg, she looked adorable.

"I need you to double check me. Take a look at the map under where the magnifying glass is lying."

She picked up the glass and examined the portion of the map below it. She looked over at Greg and grinned. "You found it! I was starting to wonder if we ever would. My God, how many searches and maps have we gone through?"

"Just enough," said Greg as Jen leaned over and kissed him.

"Have you run across Charlie Bell Well?" he asked.

She nodded. "Several times, though I've never found anything to go with the name, no pictures or even a description, except that Charlie Bell was probably a cowboy or rancher from the area but no one seems to know for sure."

"Same with me," said Greg. "There's no way of telling if Ahren's seep is connected to or is even the Charlie Bell Well, but they're sure in the same neighborhood."

"How cool! And there's even a road that takes us to the top of Charlie Bell Pass."

"In my reading," said Greg, "it doesn't look like you can't drive down through the pass, even though there's a road, but you can walk and there's all kinds of petroglyphs near the bottom. I think the area is on Cabeza Prieta Wildlife National Wildlife Refuge land, just as we anticipated."

"We haven't quite reached that bridge yet," said Jen, "but eventually we're going to have to decide if we're going to try to mine that claim or turn it over to the Refuge. I'll bet the Department of the Interior won't hesitate to mine it."

"I'll bet you're right there but they'll lease it out to a private party to do it. Our next step is to gather up the gear we need to find this claim now that we may have one landmark," said Greg. "Let's see, a compass, a rangefinder and a GPS unit would probably do it. We don't want to be too precise, I'm sure they weren't back in 1889."

"When should we go out there? I mean it's November, that would be a good time, wouldn't it, not too hot?"

"We could go this weekend if we can get the gear together," said Greg, starting to get excited.

"Remember, Jesse has the duty this weekend so he couldn't go. I don't think he'd want to miss out; besides, I doubt your knee will be ready for a hike on what is described as a moderate trail that soon. Let's talk to Jesse and Susan tonight and see what they think."

"Jesse would *not* be a happy camper if we took off up there without him, and I suppose you're right about my knee. I guess we'll just have to see how it's doing after a week of therapy."

"Make that *three* weeks of therapy. Jesse and Susan are

going out with that prospector the weekend after next. Have a little patience, the extra time will be good for your knee and, after all, the claim has been there – or not – for over a hundred and thirty years."

"Ah, damn, you're right. What's the name of that town nearby? Ajo? What's that mean in Spanish, garlic? What the hell kind of a name for a town is that?"

"Oh, don't be so grumpy, Greg. The town was probably named after the wild garlic that grows in the area according to what I read. The townspeople seem to like it so let that sleeping dog lie."

"You're right. Besides, we should see about accommodations in Ajo, shouldn't we?" I mean we should really go over there just to see what we're getting into.

Jen smiled. "As a matter of fact we should, would you do the honors while I fix dinner?"

When Jesse and Susan walked through the front door that evening, Jen couldn't contain herself, "Greg found it! We know where Ahren's Seep is!"

No less excited, Greg broke out the old territorial map and pointed out the landmark's location. Jen suggested he not mark it on the map in case it was stolen. Jesse and Susan were no less enthused, and everyone started talking at once. After a minute or so the hubbub died down and Greg asked, "The first question is do we want to camp down there or commute from Ajo?"

Susan's voice was heard over the others, "Let's camp down there!"

"Remember," cautioned Greg, "there's no water or electricity and we might not even find a level spot to camp. It's possible we could be down there for several days."

Both girls were adamant. Jesse quipped, "I think we're out-voted and it looks like *everyone* is going shopping."

After a long and expensive shopping trip to a local sporting goods store, the foursome stopped at their favorite Italian restaurant, Adolpho's, for dinner. Jesse proposed a toast after the Chianti was opened, "To a successful venture." All raised their glasses to the toast and none were aware of the photographs that were taken while they did so.

After dinner the group returned to Greg's apartment where they made plans for their impending camp out/search. Again, they had no idea that someone was photographing their cars and writing down their license plate numbers.

Jesse and Dave Gainey went shopping for a gun the next evening after Jesse was finished at the base for the day. Before they got out of Jesse's Highlander to go into the gun store, Jesse stopped Dave and said, "Dave, I'm no gun expert. I have a fair amount of experience out in the field with a variety of weapons but believe me, I'm no expert. I'm not going to tell you what gun looks good in your hand or anything like that. I'm going to nag you to pick something that is comfortable in your hand – not too big and not too small. Caliber is second to accuracy. If you can't hit your target, there's no sense in having even a .22."

"I appreciate that, Jesse, and I had come to similar conclusions myself about what gun in what caliber to choose. You're along because you're familiar with brands and points I should be looking for such as sights, magazines and so on. I'm comfortable making the final decision but two brains thinking about the objective are better than one."

Dave was more of a shopper after Jesse's heart: see what you like, buy it and get the hell out of the store. He wound up with a Glock model 22 .40 caliber just like Jesse's with a Trijicon night sight, three hi-cap magazines, a shoulder holster with mag holders on the opposite side from the weapon, a cleaning kit and four boxes of ammunition.

As they settled back in the Highlander, Jesse said, "Well, I must not have nagged enough, you bought the twin to my gun."

"Why argue with what works?" asked Dave. "The gun was very comfortable in my hand, my ego didn't require a .44 magnum and the gun has proven itself time and again. What's not to like?"

Jess chuckled. "You have a point. Okay, a week from this

Saturday morning, just like last time, right?"

"Yeah, except bring your girlfriend and her gear. I don't think I'll go back out there by myself this coming weekend, if they're going to rob the site, they've already done it and there isn't much I can do except get myself in a jam."

"I wish I could go with you this weekend but duty calls. I'll try to fly over the site in my A-10, but I won't shoot, there'd be nothing left to mine."

Dave laughed. "Okay, see you then."

Neither man saw the shadow who photographed Dave Gainey, wrote down his licenseplate number and followed him home to his apartment.

Jimbo McVey received an email containing all the information Lester Cortez had collected including five by seven glossies of all the players.

Greg and Jen spent the week moving her over to his apartment permanently. They had discussed their living together at length and agreed that there was no point in her moving back. Much of her furniture she put in storage until Jesse decided what possessions he would hang onto in Greg's apartment. Susan, of course, had a houseful of stuff so there wasn't much room left for the items of furniture he wanted to keep.

While Jesse stood his duty at the airbase, Greg and Jen drove over to Ajo, and to Charlie Bell Pass just to see what they were up against. They were glad they did, they discovered that Greg's knee wasn't as fit as they had hoped. They had started from the top of the pass where the driveable road ended but his knee started aching less than a hundred yards into the hike so they turned around and went back to his Tahoe. At least he knew what he was up against now, and had time to condition his knee.

Of Jimbo McVey or his people, they heard or saw nothing and that made Greg and Jesse nervous. The man wouldn't stand by and let them move around freely unless he had some sort of monitor on them. At their urging, everyone was especially vigilant but no one ever noticed anything suspicious.

At Greg's request, and with the approval of his surgeon, he was going to therapy twice a day, three days a week. He would *not* be left behind when his friends visited Charlie Bell Well! He had read the letter from Albert Neal to Jake Humbertson so many times, trying to read messages into it, that he almost had it memorized. Finally he gave up, there was no hidden message there that he could divine.

The girls spent every evening planning meals that were fast and simple. They didn't want to miss out on one minute of the search and were walking every morning to be ready for the hike through the mile-long pass. Even Jesse was working out. He figured he was in good enough shape but the weekend before their search would be with Dave Gainey and that would be the acid test.

Lester Cortez didn't know what to make of his quarry's activities. They weren't going anywhere or seeing anyone he didn't already know about but suddenly there was this flurry of activity. He didn't get excited, barely mentioned it in passing to his boss in one of his daily emails but wondered nevertheless.

✻✻✻✻✻

Alfredo Menendez was mystified when he was called out of his cell after his wrists were handcuffed in front and attached to a belly chain around his waist. He was led to an interview room and locked in. He sat in one of the three chairs in the small, mint green-colored room that reeked of disinfectant.

Ten minutes later he heard the door being unlocked and two men who were obviously cops entered. The door was locked behind them. Both showed Tucson Police Department credentials as they sat and the shorter, bulkier one said, "Mr. Menendez, I'm Sergeant

Salazar and this is Detective Moran. We'd like to talk to you if it's okay. But first I have to advise you of your Miranda rights."

"My lawyer told me not to talk to you," said Alfredo, curious about why they were here, and now sorry Jimbo McVey was no longer his lawyer.

"I know, and I spoke to Ms. Haub, your public defender, only an hour ago and explained that we didn't want to talk to you about your pending charges and I promised that we wouldn't. She would be here herself but she has another commitment. She told me to tell you that you might as well listen to what we have to say since it doesn't have anything to do with any crimes you might have committed."

"I'm listening."

"We're interested in what you might be able to tell us about Jimbo McVey," said Salazar.

"Why should I do that?" asked Alfredo, sniffing opportunity like a bird dog near a covey of quail.

"You have a helluva pile of felony charges stacked up against you, we might be able to make some of them go away."

"Can you get me out of here?"

"Highly unlikely, there are too many charges."

"Then what good can you do me? My attorney will cut a deal eventually and some of the charges will go away anyway."

"Not enough to keep you from doing a long stretch at the federal pen in Tucson."

"Federal pen?"

"Your attorney probably only just learned about it but the U.S. Attorney wants your cases due to the kidnapping charges and the weapon."

"That's bullshit, man."

"I'm just repeating what I was told at the prosecutor's office."

"And you can keep that from happening?"

"If you have the right information about Jimbo McVey, we

can probably do you some good." said Salazar.

"Let me talk to my attorney," said Alfredo, his mouth set in a grim line. "She'll get back to you."

CHAPTER 20

Finally it was Saturday morning. Susan was up earlier than necessary just because she was excited to go out on a prospecting foray. They met Dave Gainey at the Black Bear Diner and had breakfast. "Dave, do you have room in the back of your Trooper for Susan?" Jesse teased. "She's so excited she can't sit still and I don't know if I can drive and keep an eye on her too."

"I'll have you know, Mr. Grimes," Susan said with a prim look on her face and a turned up nose, "that I am in complete control . . . are we there yet?" She laughed and so did the men.

They had decided to take two vehicles since Dave's old Trooper wouldn't hold his mining equipment and gear for the three of them. Jesse borrowed a friend's slightly lifted four-wheel-drive pickup because he was afraid his Highlander sat too low and might be damaged by rocks and the rough road.

Dave pulled into the same wash that they had driven into two weeks before but stopped short in the soft material of the bed of the wash. He saw no one around and wanted to check to see if there were any tracks left by trespassers. He got out to look, and Jesse joined him. Both men were carrying their Glocks. They walked the wash up to the campsite but saw no evidence that anyone had been there since they left two weeks ago. Even the pile of firewood Jessse had collected on their first trip was still where he had left it. Both were relieved.

As Jesse got back in the pickup and edged them toward the campsite behind Dave's Trooper, Susan asked, "Everything okay?"

"Yep. Doesn't look like there have been any visitors and I'm really glad, so's Dave." He shifted into park and started to get back out of the vehicle. "Now the work begins."

With Susan pitching in, it didn't take long to unload both vehicles. After that, Jesse and Susan started setting up camp while Dave began lugging buckets and shovels and screens up to the dig site. It was surprisingly dusty work and, before long, Susan was sneezing and even Jesse had a coughing spell or two. The dust settled when both tents were set up and the equipment situated. They went to help Dave but found that he was already through and had begun working at the dig site.

As they approached, they saw Dave digging the soft material out of the bed of a tributary wash and dumping it into a five-gallon bucket. "This is the one I hoped those two guys didn't get into. It should show some color almost right away since the gravel downstream has been pretty productive. Jesse, can you grab a shovel and some buckets and work your way up above me in the wash and do the same thing I'm doing? We'll fill about half the buckets then stop to screen their contents into the other buckets."

"Susan, these buckets of matrix are pretty heavy and even though I have no doubt you can lift them, they have to be poured slowly through the screened top of an empty bucket to weed out the larger rocks and stuff. I think that's a little too heavy for you to do. I don't want you to overdo it and hurt something so how about Jesse and I do the screening?"

"What you can do, though, is fire up that gas-powered vacuum and start vacuuming up the pockets of gravel that are too small to get to with a shovel. Each time you finish a crevice line, dump the vacuum into a separate bucket and keep track of where they came from. That way if we discover one bucket has a lot more gold than the others, we'll know from where it came. When we run out of buckets, we'll run everything through the dry washer to further winnow out larger material. Obviously keep an eye out for nuggets and if you find something you're not sure about, call me, okay? There are a lot of minerals around here, jasper, turquoise, peridot, petrified wood, azurite and malachite to name a few. If you spot anything you like, it's yours for the taking. I'm pretty much zeroed in on gold and, as Jesse knows, part of that will be yours too."

Both young people pitched in with a will and soon there were fifteen buckets filled with screened matrix or Susan's vacuumings.

"Okay," said Dave, "let's go eat some lunch, then we'll set up the dry washer and fine tune our gold matrix."

As they ate, Dave explained how the dry washer further screened the matrix down tosand, dirt particles, small rocks and, of course, gold. After going through a dry washer, the matrix was ready for the spiral wheel concentrator which Dave explained to Susan since she had not been there to see its last demonstration.

After lunch, Dave set up the spiral wheel concentrator, aka: the panning machine, and showed Susan how it was operated. She caught on quickly and first began panning the smaller amounts she had vacuumed from the crevices. After the first three, she was discouraged, not a single particle of gold. She was looking hopefully at the catch bottle when she finished feeding the matrix into the concentrator. She clapped her hands and let out a whoop when the first gold morsels floated into the catch bottle. She had found gold! The other six buckets showed varying amounts of gold from just a few pieces to as much as an eighth of an ounce and Susan was beside herself. She was ready to go back to work with the vacuum but Dave asked that she pan the buckets they had run through the dry washer first. It was boring work feeding matrix into the panner a scoop at a time but, by the time she finished, the catch bottle had been emptied into an ounce vial once and was nearly ready to be emptied again!

The men, meanwhile, had resumed digging out the main part of the tributary wash, screening the material and getting enough buckets of matrix ready to dry wash. It was hot, dusty work even though the ambient temperature on the November day was only seventy degrees.

By the time Dave and Jesse had run the next fifteen buckets

145

of matrix through the dry washer it was getting dark. Dave called a halt and announced that they could burro the heavy buckets down to the campsite in the morning for panning. They were done for the night. They walked back down to the campsite and found that Susan had finished her panning and was in the middle of fixing something for dinner. She greeted each of them with an ice cold beer then told them to go wash their hands and face before dinner but don't use too much of "her" water!

Susan dazzled the two men with hearty Texas chili, baking powder biscuits she had baked in a Dutch oven and another ice cold brew. By the time they finished it was full dark and the lantern and a full panoply of stars was all the illumination they needed to settle in for the night. They didn't even bother lighting a campfire.

Jesse woke up with sore shoulders and back muscles from all the digging and burroing the previous day. He grunted as he rolled out of his sleeping bag and Susan asked him what was wrong.

"Yesterday was the hardest work I've done for a long time," he groaned. "If we're going to be doing a lot of this, I need to be in better condition. I run almost every day and hit the weights a couple of times a week but that didn't get me ready for *this.*"

"The only way to get in condition to do this kind of hard labor is to do it frequently," Susan commented. "I go to the gym every day, I do a lot of aerobic exercising, weights plus my martial arts training, but even I wasn't ready for slowly pouring those heavy buckets of matrix. I'm a little sore too but not as bad as you. Then again, I didn't work as physically hard as you did."

"I wonder how Dave is doing?" mused Jesse.

"Let's go find out," said Susan, "I'm hungry."

Dave was already up and had a big pot of oatmeal, cinnamon and raisins simmering on the gas stove. When he saw them emerge from their tent and walk toward him, he poured two cups of steaming coffee and handed them over.

"Good morning," Dave greeted warmly. "I trust you slept well? I sure did."

"Like the dead," moaned Jesse. "Aren't you at all sore this morning?"

"Well, I *am* a little tight around the shoulders. I guess doing twice as much as usual yesterday had something to do with it."

"Twice as much?"

Dave laughed. "Actually it's more than that but you have to look at it from a math teacher's perspective and I admit it's a little subjective. Two people can do three times what one can do alone. Three people can do about four times what one can do and we did. All we have to do today is wash these buckets of matrix then head back to Tucson. I've just about had enough for this weekend, how about you?"

"I gotta say, I now understand burro work and certainly respect what it takes to extract gold from them thar hills."

"*I* have had a great time, Dave," said Susan. "I never realized how real it is out in the desert away from everything, and I have you to thank for it so, thank you."

"I need to thank the both of you, we got four times what I could have done this weekend and I appreciate it. Besides, it gets kind of weird out here by yourself when you do it too much."

"Okay, you two, enough of the mutual admiration society, we still have a bunch of matrix to go through . . . and breakfast to eat," said Jesse with a grin.

"You know, it's a shame we couldn't put all those buckets of stuff in the back of the pickup and haul them up here. But the wash is way too rough and we'd have spilled matrix all over the place," Jesse observed.

"Yeah, I tried it a couple of times," said Dave. "Besides scraping my oil pan, the matrix did exactly what you just described – all over the inside of the Trooper."

"What about hauling the concentrator equipment and the water up to the dig site?" asked Susan.

"Again, it's just too hard on the Trooper," said Dave.

"Yeah, I suppose. Let's eat and get started," said Jesse.

After breakfast, Susan volunteered to pack up the camping gear while Dave and Jesse humped the heavy buckets of matrix down from the dig site. While Dave then helped Susan get the concentrator going, Jesse brought back the rest of the gear from the dig, then they all took turns feeding the swirling wheel.

It was worth their time. After ten buckets of matrix, they had had to empty the catch bottle twice, filling two vials. Susan couldn't get over the idea that they were extracting gold from those buckets of dirt and the gold was valuable! But the last five buckets were just dirt and sand, no gold fell into the catch bottle.

"How can that be? We were doing so well!"

"That's the way with gold panning," said Dave philosophically. "It can be hot and cold but mostly cold. We just hit a small pocket that had a lot of gold in it then there wasn't any more. I'll go back up there next time and vacuum out the crevices and will probably pick up a little more but we've exhausted that little pocket. We might as well pack up and go home."

"Will you dig farther up that wash?" asked Jesse.

"Yeah, where there was one pocket there might be two, you never know unless you give it a try."

It had been a productive thirty-six hours and Dave insisted he was well-pleased with the results, and not at all surprised that the gold had petered out. It was the nature of the beast and he tried hard to instill the concept in his two students. All told, Dave had extracted two and three quarters vials of gold from thirty buckets of matrix – a red letter day. He tried to give Jesse and Susan one of the full vials of gold but they refused, telling him they weren't out there to share his gold but to learn, and learn they did. To appease him, Jesse finally agreed to accept the partially full vial and immediately gave it to Susan, who was thrilled beyond words.

*****

After both vehicles had long departed, a Jeep Wrangler was driven slowly into the campsite. Lester Cortez got out of the vehicle and took a slow look around, noting where tents had been erected and a table set up in the soft material of the wash's bottom. He noticed the trail that led upstream about a hundred yards and walked up to examine where the trio had been digging and filtering matrix. He was confident they were mining for gold and wondered how he could determine how successful they had been.

He noticed a white post up above the bank of the wash and hiked up to it to see what it was. It was Dave Gainey's claim corner post and gave his name, address and, most importantly the date he applied for the claim. It was six months old!

When Jesse and Susan returned home, Greg and Jen were there waiting for them. Susan immediately showed her what Dave had given her which ignited both girls and they were ready then and there to head out to Charlie Bell Pass.

"Just a few more days, ladies, then you'll have a whole weekend to wander and explore and find our own placer claim."

✵✵✵✵✵

The next morning, Alfredo Menendez was again called out of his cell, handcuffed to a belly chain and led to the same interview room. Sergeant Salazar and Detective Moran were waiting for him. Salazar again gave him the Miranda rights admonishment then they got down to business.

Moran produced a recording device and set it on the table between Menendez and the two police officers.

"I don't want this recorded," said Alfredo.

"No choice – well – your choice is no recording, no deal, or we record to protect everyone involved in case someone lies. Believe it or not, some people do lie. What's it gonna be?"

Alfredo chewed his lip as he thought. *Do they already know I'm going to lie? I don't know squat about Jimbo McVey but they don't know that, and I need to feed them a real line of bullshit to get them to take me out of here.*

"Okay, go ahead and record."

Moran clicked on the recording device as Salazar started to speak, "This is Sergeant Salazar from the Tucson Police Department, the date is November 19, 2020, the time, 0915, and Detective Tom Moran and I are interviewing Alfredo Menendez at the Pima County Jail. Mr. Menendez, you are aware that this conversation is being recorded?"

Saying yes was the last thing on the planet Alfredo wanted to do but he had no choice. "Yes, I'm aware."

And you have been advised of your Miranda rights?"

"Yeah."

"Do you know Jimbo McVey?"

"Yeah."

"How do you know him?"

"We've done business together."

"What kind of business?"

"This and that."

"Can you be more specific?

"Lately we've been trying to find a gold mine."

"And how have you been doing that?"

"McVey tells me what to do and I do it."

"Like what?"

"I'm not supposed to talk about it."

"Okay. It has to do with why you're in jail now?"

"Yeah."

"Do you know of any other criminal misbehavior Mr. McVey is involved in?"

"Yeah. He's had two guys killed."

"When?"

"The first was about three years ago, a guy named Pablo Diaz. Pablo was a gangbanger and owed McVey a lot of money for drugs McVey had fronted him."

"How do you know this?"

"Pablo was a friend of mine and he told me that he owed McVey three hundred large and he didn't have no money to pay. *This all bullshit but probably true according to word on the street. No way they can prove I'm lying, Pablo's dead.*

"How was he killed?"

"Some of McVey's people took him out in the desert and shot him in the head then left

him for the buzzards and coyotes."

"How do you know this?"

"I heard about it and read it in the paper."

"So you don't have firsthand knowledge, is that right?"

"Yeah."

For a hour and twenty minutes Alfredo spun lies about all the things he had ever heard in which Jimbo McVey was involved." Some of it, what he heard on the street, was probably more true than not but Alfredo didn't know that.

As they were wrapping up the interview, Salazar asked, "We'd like to come back for another interview in the next few days. Is that okay?"

"I guess, my lawyer says it's okay. Just don't tell nobody I'm talking to you."

CHAPTER 21

Monday morning, Greg went back to work at the base on light duty between therapy sessions. At noon, he kept an appointment with his surgeon. The doctor told him that he was very pleased with Greg's progress and if he continued to improve strengthening the muscles around his knee for the next three weeks, the doctor would release him for full duty. Greg came home jubilant but found Jen in the dumps. "What's wrong? Why the long face?" he asked.

"We can't camp at Charlie Bell well," she said gloomily. "I checked on a camping permit today and Cabeza Prieta only issues permits for fourteen days in designated camping areas; Charlie Bell Well isn't one of them."

"That's okay," Greg comforted, "we'll just commute from Ajo."

"But we bought all that gear, tents, sleeping bags and all," she exclaimed.

Greg gathered her in his arms. "Do you really think this will be our only camping trip?"

She sighed. "I hope not."

"Well, it won't be. Besides, Charlie Bell Well didn't look too hospitable judging by what few pictures I've seen."

"Why didn't you say something?"

"I didn't want to disappoint you."

"That's sweet. Thank you."

"Now perk up, we have some packing, and unpacking, to do."

The week crawled by but finally it was Friday afternoon Since they weren't taking camping equipment, all their hiking gear fit easily into the back of Greg's Tahoe. They chose to take the "back" way down to Why, Arizona, on Highway 86 through the Tohono O'odham Nation and passed by Kitt Peak Observatory, Baboquivari Peak and the small community of Sells. They turned north on Highway 85 at Why, and drove the ten miles to Ajo, stopping at the Agave Grille for dinner. They checked into the La Siesta Motel and RV Resort just north of Ajo and prepared their gear for tomorrow's exploration.

They wanted to get an early start and the girls were up at six in the morning, hustling their men out of bed and into their clothes. On the way back into town, Greg stopped at the Chevron station for gas, coffee and breakfast burritos for everyone, and they continued on Highway 85 until they turned west onto Rasmussen. The road turned into gravel just at the outskirts of town and they made their way over the bumpy road for miles until they hit the *really* bumpy road that signaled the last mile to the trailhead.

Charlie Bell Pass was a gap in the Growler Mountains to the west they could see even before they arrived at the trailhead. They got out and stretched, it had been a slow, rough ride from town. They gazed out at the Growler Valley and could see all the way west to the Granite Mountains. It was desert grandeur at its finest and the foursome were impressed.

"What's the tower for?" asked Jesse.

"I read about those," said Jen. "They're an emergency phone system connected to the CBP, the Customs and Border Patrol. It was designed mainly for illegals to call in to surrender if they were out of water or had some other sort of emergency. They, of course, would be taken into custody, but their lives would be saved. Other people can use the system for emergencies too. See? It's solar powered and there's a camera"

"Yeah, I read that during the summer months, when the temperature is well over 100 every day, the CBP recovers a significant number of bodies of people who were trying to cross the desert and ran into trouble. It's a controversial subject, do you help the border crossers by putting out food, water and blankets to save their lives or do you not, thereby condemning those ill-prepared to a horrible death? The opposition maintains that by helping the illegal crossers with food and water, people are aiding and abetting the drug smugglers and they're right to some degree. I heard that some of the good "Samaritans" were even successfully prosecuted for leaving food and water in the desert."

"Man, that's a conflict I want no part of," said Susan. "Obviously there are pros and cons but I understand it can get pretty heated and I have enough conflicts in my life."

"So, let's pack up and head down the trail," said Greg, eager to see how his knee would fare. He had worked it hard and the improvement was apparent, he just hoped it was enough.

The foursome started down the fairly steep, rock-strewn trail, classified as "moderate" in the literature.. In the first three quarters of a mile, the trail dropped almost three hundred feet and it was steep, rocky going. After that, it began to level out considerably and the hiking was easier. Another three-quarters of a mile and the windmill at Charlie Bell Well appeared along with many boulders covered with desert varnish and countless Hohokam petroglyphs from hundreds or thousands of years past according to those who professed to know what they were talking about. One theory was that the petroglyphs were a sort of bulletin board near a source of water initially called Ahren's Seep by the first white men to discover it.

"Just where exactly is Ahren's Seep?" asked Jesse of his friend.

"I never found the answer to that question so I'm going to take a SWAG (scientific wild-assed guess) and say that someone, maybe Charlie Bell, whoever he was, dug or drilled right down into the seep and tinaja and made a well out of it. I'm thinking we need to measure from the Charlie Bell Well itself," Greg replied.

Once the got to the well, they shucked off their day packs in the shade, but kept their hiking sticks. Greg retrieved a portable range finder from his pack. He took up a position with his back to the well with the range finder out in front of him. He sighted northwest until he spotted a a particularly tall grove of ocotillo cactus about five hundred feet up the hill. Jesse hiked up the steep, rocky wash and finally clambered up the bank to the grove. He wrapped bright orange surveyor's tape around it. Everyone slowly hiked up to the landmark, saving their energy for the search ahead. They spread out about twenty feet apart in a line from the ocotillo and began walking a clockwise pattern looking for the first landmark in the metes and bounds description, "a large boulder with many pictures scratched in it, the biggest being a sun symbol". It was difficult keeping station in the line while dodging rocks and untangling themselves from creosote bushes obstructing their way.

After fifteen minutes of struggling through the terrain, Susan called out that she thought she had found it. Everyone held position until Greg could work his way to her and confirm the landmark, which he did. The sun symbol was obviously the largest petroglyph on the boulder. Greg returned to the Jesse's ocotillo grove, unwrapped the surveyor's tape from around the cactus, and carried it over to the sun stone and wrapped it around the boulder Jake Humbertson had probably described in his application for a claim.

They laboriously repeated the process for the next landmark, a solitary snake carved into a large flat rock about two hundred fifty feet distant from the boulder with the sun etched in it. They quickly located the snake slab but, not surprisingly, had trouble locating the third landmark, a mesquite tree along the bank of the main wash. At least they were now going downhill. "I wish they had just picked another boulder, it stands to reason that the tree would be long gone in a hundred thirty years," groused Jesse.

"Let's go down in the wash and walk along the bank a ways," Jen suggested. "There might be a stump or roots still showing."

With Greg staying at the slab with the snake on it, the other three slipped and slid their way down the hill and into the wash. An examination of the bank of the wash revealed nothing that anyone could point to and say had been a mesquite tree.

Though they were unsuccessful, Jen found an interesting rock she thought might be a gold nugget.

"What do you think?" she asked the others hopefully.

"It sure looks like a gold nugget to me," said Susan, looking closely at the object. "It's obviously smaller than the one Greg found but it sure seems to be of the same material. I'm certain it's not iron pyrite or fool's gold because the edges aren't sharp like pyrite would be. Jen, I think you found our first gold."

Smiling, Jen put it in her pocket. "Let's see, ten percent of that amounts to about a dollar fifty, I'm rich!"

After conferring with Greg, they agreed that where five hundred feet from the snake landmark intersected with the bank of the wash would suffice as the last claim corner. It wasn't exactly two hundred fifty feet from this landmark to the well but close enough. Jesse drove an iron stake into the side of the wash and wrapped bright surveyor's tape around it.

They felt they had pretty much established an accurate perimeter of the Cactus Wren claim. Not surprisingly it encompassed a wide wash that collected from many tributaries.

"What I think we should do next is see if we can find that cache of tools," said Greg, panting from his hike down the hill. "It may save us buying a bunch of equipment and it'll confirm that we're at the right place,"

"The letter said, 'the usual place,' huh?" questioned Jesse. "It would be nice if we knew where they had been mining. The tool cache probably isn't far from there."

"Makes sense," said Susan, then she looked over at Jen and smiled. "Keep your eyes peeled as we walk up the wash *again*, okay?"

Four pairs of eyes examined the banks of the main wash as

they struggled upstream farther than the upper boundaries of the claim. Four pairs of eyes found not only nothing in the way of a cache of equipment but no evidence in the tributary washes of any digging or tailings.

It was past noon by the time they finished examining the wash and they stopped for lunch in what shade a large mesquite tree offered. It was not a hot day but the foursome had been doing a lot of hiking and were ready for a drink and a rest.

"Maybe they had a hollowed out a place into the bank of the wash," said Jen. "We should probably walk the upper banks of the wash too just to be sure. That will enable us to look farther up the tributary washes too. I guess we should probably shoot some pictures while we're at it in case we miss something."

"That means a whole lot more up and down hiking through those smaller washes," Jesse observed as he munched on a sandwich.

"You know," said Greg, "we might have been smarter to invest in a drone."

"I was just thinking the same thing," said Jesse, "that would save us a lot of hiking both in and out and up and down these washes. And we need to examine the side washes better too."

"If we don't find something on this trip, maybe we'll go shopping for one when we get back. I assume they're expensive?" asked Greg.

"I've heard they can be," said Jesse, "I think they range from around a hundred dollars for a cheap one to several hundred or even thousands depending on what you want it to do."

"No strafing or bombing drones, you guys," said Susan with a grin.

"Okay, okay, surveillance only," quipped Greg. "You know, after looking around a little, I'm kind of glad we're staying in town. I wonder where the miners had their camp?"

"Greg?" asked Jen, "How's your knee holding up?"

"Pretty well. I've had a couple of twinges on uneven ground

when I wasn't paying attention where I was walking, but by and large I'm doing fine."

"Do you think going up the banks of the wash is too much?"

"Nope, I'm doing fine but thanks for asking."

"He'd never tell you even if his leg was about to fall off," said Jesse. I've never seen anyone with a higher pain threshold."

"I'd say something if it was too much," said Greg, "there's more at stake than a paltry gold mine. Flying is involved, after all!"

"Just don't push your luck, cowboy, only you know when it's time to stop," cautioned Jesse. "Is everyone through with lunch?"

"Okay, up the banks of the wash we go," said Susan, rising from her rock with a big sigh.

They started up the rough, rocky and often brushy edges of he wash. What they couldn't go through, they went around and had to shuffle down into the tributary washes and clamber up the other side. It was tiring work and after an hour and a half, everyone was sweating and breathing hard but had found nothing.

"Damn these guys are sneaky!" Jesse exclaimed as they paused to catch their breath. You'd think 'the usual place' would be obvious."

"Yeah . . . in 1889," puffed Greg. "Gotta remember a lot of weather has fallen on this area in over a century. Shall we switch sides at the top and come back down or come down in the wash?"

"I vote we do the same thing going back down the other side," said Susan, "if we're going to do this, we should do it right."

No one disagreed so about a hundred feet beyond the upper claim boundary, they switched sides and headed back down.

By the time they all got back to the well, they were truly bushed. No one dissented when Greg suggested they call it a day; after all, they still had a three-mile hike *up* the pass to the trailhead.

All were looking forward to reaching the Tahoe and the extra water they had left in a cooler. Little was said on the trip back to Ajo, nor did they pay much attention to the nondescript four by four pickup they passed on their way back to Ajo. They barely noted that the vehicle was headed out toward the trailhead.

Lester Cortez simply ignored the oncoming Tahoe as he drove out to the trailhead but he knew who was in it. He had his drone in the back seat under a blanket and wasn't worried the occupants of the SUV would notice anything about him, the vehicle or its contents.

When he arrived at the trailhead, he assembled the drone and launched it. He only had about forty minute's flight time and he wanted to see what his targets had been doing. All he knew was that they had spent most of the day somewhere down the Charlie Bell Pass trail and he hoped to spot any evidence of activity.

The drone was a good one he had used on other operations and Cortez was confident that its four-mile range would be sufficient. He flew down the trail into the pass and noticed where the terrain began to level out. He noted nothing of interest and continued down the trail until he got to the windmill. Almost immediately he spotted the surveyor's tape wrapped around the two rocks above and a stake driven in the bank of a wash. Had they found the Cactus Wren claim or was this a ruse to lead someone away from the true location in the Dome Rock Mountains where they were already mining?

✳✳✳✳✳

"I don't know no addresses," whined Alfredo Menendez, lying his ass off. "I can point out his drug houses and the gambling places if you could get me out of here for a while. I even know where some of McVey's girls live but that ain't gonna do you no good with me in here."

Frustrated, Salazar swore under his breath as he started thinking of a way to check Menendez out of the jail for a few hours.

CHAPTER 22

Jesse drove them directly to the motel where everyone availed themselves of showers and clean clothes. "Yeah," said Jen as she pulled on a clean pair of jeans, "staying at a motel was the right decision."

It was dark when they set out to find a place for dinner. They wound up back at the Agave Grille and, over a bottle of wine, discussed the day's activities. "Well, I think we accomplished what we set out to do, except for finding the tools. That still seems like our first priority for the same reasons as before," said Greg. "It also seems to me that if we find their tools, we'll be that much closer to finding where they were working." He stopped suddenly and looked around him to make sure no one was listening, but there were only a couple of patrons sitting at the bar.

"I guess we'd better be a little more circumspect in our conversations in public, never know who might be listening. Anyway, as I was saying, I can't imagine them hauling their tools all the way to the top or bottom of the wash or even up the pass every day if that was where they were working. They'd stash them someplace closer."

"Unless there were marauding Indians in the vicinity who would also steal if they couldn't kill," Susan commented.

"Point well taken, and he did say in the letter they had stashed them to avoid theft," said Greg.

"What do you think about getting a metal detector to go over some of the areas we covered today to see if we can get a hit on some metal – not necessarily gold?" asked Jesse.

"Great idea, Jesse," said Jen, "I wish we had thought of it before today. It would have saved us a bunch of work."

"But where would we find a metal detector to rent in Ajo? It

160

doesn't make a helluva sense to drive all the way to Phoenix to rent one; we might just as well rent one in Tucson, at least it would be easier to return," said Greg.

"That's at least a five or six-hour round trip," said Jesse, "maybe on this trip it isn't such a good idea."

"There's gotta be mining museums here, wouldn't it be worth a try to ask someone who is familiar with mining in the area?"

They asked their waitress about mining museums in town. Yes, there were two but she strongly recommended going to the one on the edge of the copper mine pit in town and talking to a man named Bob Hightower. "What Hightower doesn't know about mining isn't worth knowing."

They were at the small museum on the rim of the New Cornelia Mine the next morning. Unfortunately it didn't open until ten and they were there shortly after eight.

"We might as well go have a good breakfast. I heard some people talking about a place called Granny's in Why. It's supposed to have some good Mexican breakfast items along with American fare," suggested Jen. As no one had a better suggestion, off to Why they went. The *chilaquiles* exceeded expectations and no one went away hungry.

They took their time driving back to Ajo and arrived at the museum at just about the time Bob Hightower and his wife were opening up for business. He welcomed the foursome into the museum and they took the tour before getting down to business. They found Hightower to have an encyclopedic knowledge of mining during the era of the New Cornelia mine which had been shut down since 1983.

Greg finally got around to asking Hightower about the availability of a metal detector.

The old curator thought for a moment then decided. "I have one I'll loan you as long as you take care of it. I'm probably too old to ever use it again but it's like an old friend that I'd like to see cared for with respect. Probably ought to charge it up before you try to use it, it has sat for quite a while."

Greg gave Hightower one of his business cards and the man was suitably impressed. "I see you guys flying A-10s over the town all the time and always say that the sound of your engines means freedom for the rest of us. Thank you for your service.

"Come with me," said Hightower to Greg as he hobbled toward a store room with the aid of his walker. He opened a door into the back and reached around a corner, drawing forth a canvas bag with "Minelab" emblazoned on it.

"This used to be state of the art a few years ago, but I've quit keeping up with new developments in the industry so the newer ones might have more features. This is a good, solid metal detector that should do the job. What are you going to use it for, by the way?"

"We thought we'd do some detecting out along the *El Camino del Diablo* (the Devil's Highway), see if we can find any interesting relics on our way to Yuma," Greg lied. He hated to lie to the old gentleman but certainly didn't want to admit he was going to use the detector to break the law across several fronts.

"It should work just fine for that. Do you need the owner's manual?" he asked.

"Every model is a little different, probably would be a good idea."

Hightower retrieved a booklet from a shelf in the storage room and handed it to Greg. "This is pretty user friendly, hopefully you won't have to spend all your time studying it instead of detecting."

"Thank you, Mr. Hightower, I promise we'll take good care of it."

As they climbed back into Greg's Tahoe, Greg muttered, "I *hate* lying to that guy."

Jen hugged his arm and said, "It won't hurt him . . . as long as you don't break his machine!"

"That won't happen," Greg vowed.

162

Metal detector problem solved, they stopped at Olsen's IGA, had some sandwiches made up for lunch and bought some snacks to go with them. They still had plenty of water from the previous day.

As they bounced and shuddered their way back out to the Charlie Bell Pass trailhead, they discussed the best way to use the metal detector. It was unanimous that they begin their search by combing the upper banks of the wash. That meant a lot more hiking but they had assumed there would be plenty of that from the beginning.

"While you guys scan with the detector, why don't Jen and I go up and remove the surveyor's tape. That stuff is pretty visible and would look suspicious to anyone else hiking in this area," suggested Susan. Both men nodded their agreement and the girls started up the bottom of the main wash.

As Bob Hightower had promised, the metal detector was user friendly and both Greg and Jesse got the hang of it quickly. They passed it back and forth as they worked their way along the upper right bank of the main wash and up and down through the tributary arroyos. The detector remained frustratingly silent. When they got to the top of the claim, they stopped for a breather and some water.

"Is it possible we're not doing this right?" asked Jesse.

"Pretty hard to screw up running one of these things judging by what it said in the book," Greg replied. "It stands to reason there won't be much metal out here except what we're looking for."

"Well, it's sure as hell a hum so far!" groused Jesse as he took the detector and started working his way down the left bank of the main wash. They switched back and forth and were about a third of the way down the wash when the detector gave off with a loud series of chirps. The girls were just down below, having gathered up all the surveyor's tape and were still heading back down.

"Did you find something?" asked Susan.

"Can't tell yet, it's about halfway to the bottom from up here.

Do you see anything? It's right below us," said Jesse who was running the instrument at the time. He had to raise his voice to be heard over incessant chirping of the instrument.

"Give us a second to get a little closer," said Susan as both girls laboriously dodged around large rocks and uprooted trees to get below the men.

"Wait a minute," cried Jen, "I see something." She bent down and reached into a bush . . . and came out with a rusted tin can. "Here it is," she called to the men, "here's our treasure."

Greg laughed, Jesse scowled and said, "Crap!"

Not twenty feet farther down the wash, the instrument chirped again. This time Greg had the machine. "Probably more trash," he called out to the girls who were farther down the wash. "Whatever it is looks like it might be all the way down in the bottom. You girls want to come back up and check it or shall we come down off the bank?"

"We'll check it," said Susan, "just give us a minute to get back up there."

Ten minutes went by before Jen and Susan were able to struggle between TV-sized rocks to the location Greg indicated.

"There's a big snarl of brush down . . . wait, the bank is undercut," said Jen. Susan joined her and they pulled several old, dried out mesquite and palo verde roots out of their way. It was silent for a few seconds then Jen cried, "It's the tools, we found the tools!"

Both men came scrambling down the bank kicking up dust and a shower of dirt and rocks. "Jeez, you guys," said Susan, coughing up dust, "you wouldn't have come down that fast if one of us had broken a leg!"

Jesse, after brushing himself off, looked at her and grinned as he said, "Would too."

"Hey!" called Greg, "Come take a look at this." They all hunkered down just outside the undercut in the bank where the miners had stashed their supplies and equipment. They could see boxes of canned goods, pick axes, shovels, iron bars and a variety of matrix screening tools. There were gold pans, kitchen utensils, an axe, a keg of nails and a few things they didn't even recognize. Greg was the first to notice the leather dispatch packet tucked between two of the boxes of canned goods.

"What's that?" he asked, pointing to the leather pouch.

"Looks like an oversize wallet," said Jesse, reaching for it.

Surprisingly, the packet was dried out and crackly but intact. Jesse plucked it out of the pile and backed away from the undercut so everyone could see and there would be some light.

"What's in it?" asked Susan eagerly, as Jesse began to untie the bindings. He finished and folded open the crackling leather pouch. Inside was one folded page, addressed to Jake Humbertson in a very shaky hand that in no way resembled Albert Neal's previous letter:

May 14, 1889

Jake,

Not much time. My leg is infected and they say gangrene has set in. That means I'm going to die, and soon judging by the awful smell and the pain. You need to know that we buried the gold to the right of that rock where you found the rock carving that looked like a man's hand. It's all there and it's all yours.

The Cactus Wren is played out. Until the Indians showed up we were working the upper washes and finding nothing. As you know the side wash where we found most of the gold is played out too – all we got was sand and dirt.

Don't stick around, it's too dangerous. The gold is safe, no one knows where it is except you and me and soon that will be just you.

Lieutenant Capps says he has to take this letter now. He's going to sneak up to where the gear is and leave it there for you. Be careful and God bless.

Albert

Everyone stood there stunned for several moments. Gold? Greg stood, thoughtful, for several minutes after the others had recovered and were talking among themselves.

"I don't know about you guys," said Jesse, "but I'm going to grab a shovel and go looking for some gold." He moved past the girls and went to reach for one of the shovels in the cache.

"Wait a minute, Jesse," said Greg, putting his hand on his friend's arm. "I have an idea."

"A better idea than digging for gold?" Jesse asked, mystified.

"It has to do with Jimbo McVey," said Greg, the idea still not completely formed in his mind. "Let's think this through. McVey knows we have the same information he has about this claim and he assumes we're trying to find it. He's sitting back waiting for us to find it then he'll move in and take over. But McVey doesn't know about Albert Neal's second letter, he doesn't know there is gold, much less that *we* know where the gold is . . . or will soon enough."

"But what if McVey decides to wait until we 'mine' the gold?" asked Susan, catching on at once.

"We have to figure out a way to make him think it's his idea to jump the gun and move on us before, say, we turn the claim over to the government," said Greg with a shrug.

"I almost wish that idiot, Alfredo, was out of jail. It would be much easier to convince him than McVey," said Jen.

"In the meantime, I think we'd be smart not to disturb anything in the cache. The gold - we assume – has endured for a hundred and thirty years, it can wait a while longer and so can we."

"I think we'd better destroy that second letter," said Jesse, "if it gets into McVey's hands, the game is over."

"If we're being followed, which I think is a good possibility," said Greg, "leaving the surveyor's tape out over night was probably an inadvertently good thing to do as was taking it down today. If McVey's people are on us, they already know we're looking down here. I haven't heard any aircraft and we might or might not hear a drone if it's high enough, so unless they have people on the ground, I don't think they can watch us, only what we've done if we leave any evidence."

"Do we want them to know we found the cache of supplies and tools?" asked Susan.

"I think so, that way we've confirmed that this is the right claim," said Greg, looking askance at the others. They all nodded.

"How?" asked Greg.

"We could leave a shovel handle sticking out from the overhang," said Jen.

"I wonder if that pickup that came in as we were leaving was our watcher," mused Jesse.

"Good possibility," said Greg, "there's been no one else in here either day so far, that we know of."

"Okay, Jesse, do you want to do the honors with one of their shovels, under our supervision, of course?" asked Susan.

Jesse stepped past Greg then crouched down under the undercut. He grabbed the the handle of the closest shovel and pulled it out toward him then lay it on the bed of the wash with about two feet sticking out past the snarl of branches.

"Perfect," said Susan, "now let's go find some gold."

They fanned out next to the seep and began working their way up the hillside along the wash, looking for the boulder with the hand etched in it. Jen found it within the first fifty feet.

"Here it is, you guys!" she called. The image was etched in the desert varnish on the stone and, though crude, clearly depicted a man's spread hand.

When the others had gathered around it, Jesse said, "Well there's no doubt that's what it is.", "I guess this is as good as X marks the spot, huh?" He straightened up and shifted his pack to one shoulder so he could reach in and retrieve a folding shovel.

"Jesse, I'll be helping you in a minute but be careful to scrape away the surface matter from where we're going to dig. That way we can brush it back over the spot after we fill in the hole when we're done," said Greg, retrieving his own shovel.

The material to the right of the boulder wasn't hardpan but it was packed solid and digging was hard. At one point they debated getting a pick from the cache but decided a little harder digging was better than disturbing the tools. The two men dug hard for about thirty minutes, down barely a foot below the surface, when Jesse's shovel struck something that didn't quite sound like a rock.

Carefully, Jesse unearthed the stoppered neck of a bottle . . . hen another and another. The bottles were grouped close together and, as the men widened the hole, more bottles appeared. When the dirt and rocks were cleared away down to the shoulders of the bottles, they counted sixteen old whiskey bottles.

"Great, they buried their booze over the top of the gold," said Jesse as he reached down to pull a bottle from the ground. He grunted then pulled harder, finally pulling the bottle from the material surrounding it. Clearly it was heavy since Jesse was using two hands to pull it out of the ground.

"Jesus, this thing has to be full of gold!" he exclaimed once he got it out of the ground.

Greg pulled up another bottle, finding the same resistance or weight. "You're right," he said, after he had brushed the dust from the other bottle. The girls gathered closer and stared down at the two bottles.

"Where are we going to hide sixteen fifths of gold?" Jen wondered out loud. "How much do you think they weigh, Greg?"

"I don't know, at least as much as a twenty-pound sack of flour."

"That's going to be a lot of weight to be packing up the hill, amigos," Jesse observed.

"I don't mind, do you?" asked Greg and they all laughed, but it was a restrained laugh; everyone was in awe of what they had found.

They just stood there staring until Greg got them going again. "Okay, girls, why don't you go out to the trail and bring back some medium-sized rocks we can use for backfill under the overburden so it's not obvious someone's been digging here. Jesse and I will load everyone's pack, two for each of the girls and six for Jesse and me."

"Why don't you not kill us off by trying to haul that much up the hill at once?" asked Susan. "Even if you made it three each for the girls and five each for you guys that's simply too much weight for any of us to lug all the way to the top. Wouldn't it be better if we made two, or even three trips? I know that's a lot of hiking but that's a lot of weight."

"Okay," said Greg, "Let's do it."

They all set to work and in less time than it took to find the gold, the packs were loaded and no one could tell anyone had ever dug near the rock with the hand on it.

They were long, sweaty hikes back up the grade to the Tahoe, but by taking it slowly and reducing the load, the foursome made it both times without incident. There was an anxious moment when they crested the top of the pass the first time, afraid someone might be waiting for them but the coast was clear.

It was a quiet ride back to Ajo, everyone was tired and thinking not about what they would do with the gold, but how to keep it.

*****

Salazar and Moran sat across from Assistant U.S. Attorney, Kelly Greenward in his office in Tucson. Salazar had made the appointment after his last interview with Menendez. Alfredo had convinced him that he could show the officers many of the places where Jimbo McVey conducted his criminal enterprise and, though there was always a risk taking a prisoner out of jail, he deemed the pros outweighed the cons. Besides, Menendez didn't seem that smart or that aggressive.

169

"I don't know," said the attorney, this is irregular to say the least. You're sure the defense attorney is onboard with this?"

"Yes," said Salazar, "I confirmed it on the phone coming over here."

"You want me to go into the judge's chambers, and submit a motion ordering you to take, um, Alfredo Menendez out of the jail for up to four hours while he points out places of interest in a Continuing Criminal Enterprise? Have you considered the shit storm it will cause if you lose him and the press hears about it?"

"That's why we've arranged for the U.S. Marshalls to do the actual transport and security," said Salazar.

"I see."

"This is an extraordinary chance to obtain significant evidence against Jimbo McVey's CCE and opportunities like this don't come along every day."

"Jimbo McVey, huh? No one has gotten even close to him in the seven years I've been here," mused Greenward. "Okay, I'll take your motion before the judge."

"*Please* don't forget to have it sealed afterward . . . to protect the informant. McVey would have him killed in a New York minute if he found out about this, and if he couldn't reach him, he'd go after the informant's family."

"Okay, I'll get back to you after I see the judge."

CHAPTER 23

Lester Cortez didn't want to risk the occupants of the Tahoe seeing his pickup two days in a row so he waited for them to leave the trailhead by parking almost all the way back to Ajo where they couldn't see him. When he saw a dust plume in the road heading his way, he backed under an ironwood tree and hunkered down in the seat so he could just see through the steering wheel over the dash and through the tree. Sure enough, it was the Tahoe slowly making its way back to town, the driver trying to avoid the worst of the rocks and bumps.

He waited just long enough for their vehicle to disappear from sight, then he started the pickup and headed for Charlie Bell Pass. This time he was going to hike down the pass and have a look around. He parked at the trailhead, unpacked his drone and headed down the trail. When he got down to where the terrain evened out, he launched the drone and used it to fly over the claim site once again. He saw immediately that the surveyor's tape was gone but nothing else appeared left behind or out of place.

He descended and flew the drone up the length of the main wash from Charlie Bell Well to about where he remembered the upper limits of the claim being, still not seeing anything out of the ordinary. He descended still lower, until all he could see was the bed of the wash and flew slowly back toward the well. This time he noticed a branch sticking out from a snarl of branches along the left bank that looked a little too straight to be a branch. He finished his flight and stowed the drone then decided to hike up the wash himself to look around, especially at that branch that looked too straight to be a branch.

He couldn't see the branch until he was almost on top of it

and, sure enough, it was the weathered handle of a tool. He ducked under some of the snarl where the other end disappeared and caught a glimpse of a shovel blade. He eased under the snarl a little more and discovered the undercut in the bank and the pile of equipment and supplies. Ever cautious, he retrieved a powerful flashlight from his pack and looked at the cache in better light. This was not a pile of tools and supplies that had recently been put here. Cortez could see where water had run through the tools and up against the pile of boxes leaving a residue of dried dirt and debris. So this *was* the Cactus Wren claim!

He wondered if the people he was watching had discovered the cache as well and assumed they had, considering how many times they had had to have gone up and down the wash searching for it. He debated bringing back an artifact for McVey but decided against it, concerned that they might notice and learn that someone was following them.

He decided to head back to town instead. He would give McVey his daily update and let him decide what to do next.

As he pulled his pickup up to Rasmussen and Highway 85 in Ajo, Cortez saw the Tahoe southbound on Highway 85. Curious, he waited for a couple of cars to pass by in the same direction and pulled out behind them. He watched the Tahoe make the left ninety-degree bend in the highway then immediately turn right into the nearly empty parking lot of a restaurant. On impulse, Cortez turned left into the parking lot of a barber shop and parked. He watched the foursome emerge from the Tahoe and enter the restaurant. He decided to do a little eavesdropping since they didn't know him. He left his sunglasses on and pulled down his ballcap.

"I'm telling you that's the same pickup that we saw coming from the pass the other day," said Susan as they walked toward the restaurant.

"If it is, so what? We can't just shoot him," said Jesse as they watched the man walk across the highway toward the restaurant.

"Just follow my lead when he sits down," said Susan, a crafty glint in her eye.

Cortez walked into the restaurant and took a table close by. He sat with his back to them and ordered a beer and a sandwich, then just acted like he was working on his phone.

"I hate the idea of going back to work tomorrow," said Susan. "It has been such a productive weekend."

"As the proverb goes, all good things must come to an end, baby," said Jesse, taking a drink from his bottle of beer.

"I know, but we accomplished so much, confirming the claim and all. Now we have to let the people at the Wildlife Refuge take over and mine it."

"It's pretty small potatoes, Susan," said Greg. The Refuge might report it to the Department of the Interior but I'd be surprised if anyone did anything about it."

"What a waste. Jake Humbertson and his pals should be rolling over in their graves at the thought. They already hauled forty-two ounces out of that little claim. God knows what they would have recovered if the Indians hadn't intervened."

"It's out of our hands; I'm sure not willing to risk my career and bust my ass mining it, then have the feds confiscate everything." said Jesse, disgust tingeing his voice.

"In reality, it was taken out of our hands the minute we learned it was in the Cabeza Prieta National Wildlife Refuge," said Jen. "We just didn't realize we couldn't mine it until after I read the regulations."

The talk diminished after their food came. Cortez pretended to still be fascinated with his phone, making up text messages to himself then erasing them until his food came.

When they finished eating, Greg got up to pay the bill and the others prepared to leave. "So are you going to write the letter to the Refuge?" Jen asked Susan.

"Yeah," said Susan, "tomorrow or the next day. I'll write a

cover letter and enclose the original letter from Albert Neal and the other documents plus the map that Greg drew so they can find it."

Jen sighed. "I guess it was fun while it lasted, right?"

"I'm not going to miss digging and screening like we did with Dave Gainey just for the practice," said Jesse as he opened the door for the girls.

As Greg paid the bill, he asked the waitress if she knew where Bob Hightower lived. She did not, but told Greg that the Hightowers came into dinner once in a while and she was well familiar with them. Greg explained that they had Hightower's metal detector and couldn't return it since the museum was closed.

The waitress, Wanda, said, "Oh, just leave it here, we'll give it to Bob the next time he comes in."

Greg finished with the bill and said, "It's out in my truck, I'll run out and get it." He walked past his friends and out to the Tahoe where he retrieved the metal detector and brought it inside to Wanda. He handed her two fifty dollar bills and asked that she give them to Hightower for the use of the instrument.

"You can be sure he'll get his metal detector and his money," said Wanda with a smile, and Greg was sure that would be the case.

Greg joined the others and they walked out to the Tahoe and Greg headed them back toward Tucson.

"Well, either we tipped him off big time that we're onto him," said Susan after they were all back in the SUV, "or we hooked him deep. If it's the latter, we should be getting some action before tomorrow."

"That guy didn't even look at us once," said Jen.

Cortez hurriedly wolfed down the rest of his sandwich, left ample money on the table to pay his bill, then hustled out the door and across the street to his pickup.

"I think I just confirmed he's our shadow," said Greg. "He just came running across the road, then the pickup pulled out going our direction."

"What's he going to do, follow us all the way back to

Tucson?" asked Jen.

"That's what I would do if I was him; otherwise he has no way of knowing where we're going," Jesse said, turning to look behind them.

"We go home," said Greg calmly, "and wait. Jesse and Susan? Do you want to stay with us or call it a night and head home? For what it's worth? I'd be surprised if he didn't know where you live too."

Jesse looked over at Susan and she nodded. "I believe we'll be staying with you. Safety in numbers. Everyone has their piece?" All nodded heads in the affirmative."

"Um, I'm sure everyone has thought about it, but what should we do with the bottles in the back?" asked Jen.

"For the time being, I don't think we have much of a choice but to take them into the apartment for now. We can't leave them in the Tahoe," said Greg. "Susan, you found some gold buyers, right? Maybe we should see how much they're prepared to buy at one time."

"Since you're so freshly back to work, Greg," said Jesse, "I probably ought to take tomorrow off and stay with Jen until we get the matter of the gold resolved."

"That would be greatly appreciated, Jesse," said Jen, relief in her voice.

"And it's all agreed that if we get a visit this evening, we're careful to keep poker faces on, and volunteer nothing. We don't want to make this guy suspect anything. If we can convince him he's scared us off, I think we have a chance of being free of this thing."

"What a relief that would be!" said Susan with conviction.

"What else?" asked Greg.

"Yeah," said Jesse. "I've been meaning to bring it up for a while now and just keep getting distracted. Jen is getting ten percent of whatever gold we recover, right?" There were nods of agreement around the inside of the cab of the Tahoe.

"I think she deserves a twenty-five percent share. Considering what she has gone through since she signed on I think she more than deserves a full share. Besides that, she's putting up with Greg!"

There was no hesitation, no thinking the suggestion over, everyone affirmed the motion immediately and Jen got a hug from Greg, and Susan reached up front to squeeze her hand.

"I'm sorry this didn't come up sooner, Jen. You've deserved a full share since the first time you were robbed, I can't think of why it took so long to discuss this," said Susan, looking at her friend.

"I honestly hadn't given it a thought. I've been so caught up in the hunt that, like Jesse, I've been distracted. But thank you all," said Jen. No one could see the tears in her eyes but her voice carried the sentiment. "Jeez you guys, now I feel like I need to go shoot someone to deserve it!"

"No, no, don't," said Susan with a laugh, "we'll settle for your kicking the crap out of one of the robbers!"

"Here here," said the two men in unison.

They arrived at Greg and Jen's apartment a little after 6 PM and quickly unloaded their cargo, still in the backpacks, into the apartment. They all wanted to take a lot closer look but were afraid they'd be interrupted and maybe even discovered.

✶✶✶✶✶

"What?" rumbled Jimbo McVey as he answered his very private phone.

"It's me."

"Yes?"

"They found the claim."

"How can you be sure? They were screwing around with two claims."

"They found the cache of equipment and supplies in the one outside of Ajo. They were at the other claim just for practice."

"How do you know that?"

"I heard them talking. They also plan to send a letter to the Wildlife Refuge along with the letter from the miner, the other documents, and a map of where the claim is."

"Goddamnit! Can you stop them?"

"I can waste them."

"No! I don't want this turning messy and complicated. Do you think you can scare them?"

"Two of them are combat pilots, what do you think?"

"Buy 'em off if you have to, but only if you have to."

"You do know this claim is on the Cabeza Prieta Wildlife Refuge and mining is prohibited there?"

"Let me worry about that. Just get those four pains in the ass out of the way without generating a bunch of headlines and a huge investigation."

"What's my limit?"

"Use your own discretion but don't be generous."

"I'll be in touch," said Cortez. When he hung up the phone he began to laugh. He drove the rest of the way back to Tucson laughing to himself.

When Cortez arrived in Tucson, he went straight to the apartment on Haughton. Not surprisingly the Tahoe was there along with Jesse's Highlander. After debating the idea, he left his Beretta in the pickup. This was not supposed to be a violent contact but if it turned into one he would improvise as he had been trained to do.

He knocked on the door and moments later the porch light came on and Greg answered it.

Before Greg could speak, Cortez started in: "Captain Miller, my name is Lester Cortez and I wonder if I could discuss a business matter with you and your friends? I won't take long and it will worth your while."

Greg recognized Cortez right away from the restaurant,

nodded at his words, and opened the door to allow him entrance. "Everyone, this is Lester Cortez, he says he wants to discuss a business matter with us. Do you know my friends, Mr. Cortez, or shall I introduce them?"

"No, that's alright, I recognize everyone." He stood there awkwardly for a moment until Greg motioned him to a chair. "I'll jump right into this: I represent someone who is interested in the Cactus Wren gold claim and the . . ."

"You mean Jimbo McVey?" Susan interrupted.

"You're well-informed," Cortez noted coolly. "Yes, Jimbo McVey is very interested in acquiring the rights to that claim."

"Even though it's on Cabeza Prieta Wildlife Refuge land and can't legally be mined?" asked Jen.

"Girls, let the man talk. I'm sure we'll get our turn," said Greg.

"Thank you," said Cortez, shooting a grateful glance at Greg. "As I was saying, Mr. McVey is interested in exclusive rights to the Cactus Wren claim. I pointed out the same issue to him as you just did, Ms. Belle Isle, and he told me to let him worry about that so I shall. I suggest you do the same; if he wants to take the claim to court and try to win the mining rights to the claim, who am I to object?"

"Now, clearly you four have an interest in the claim as well. Mr. McVey wonders what it would take to induce you to relinquish your interest and that's basically why I'm here."

It was obvious Jesse wanted to speak but held his tongue.

Cortez looked around the room at the four young people with his eyebrows raised.

Jesse actually raised his hand! "Mr. Grimes, you have a question?" asked Cortez.

"More in the way of a statement. We will *not* be intimidated, nor will we submit under the threat of violence as your predecessor learned."

"I in no way suggested that you would, and I'm not here to

offer more of that lunacy. Mr. Menendez was acting independently and his actions were in no way condoned by Mr. McVey. He wants a more, shall we say, civilized, resolution."

"What, exactly, does he want?" asked Greg.

"Your promise that you'll never speak of this claim again to anyone except among yourselves, and take no action against Mr. McVey if you perceive that his actions *vis a vis* the claim don't appear completely to comply with the letter of the law. In other words, you won't say anything to anyone if you learn that he's trying to mine the claim."

"Mr. McVey also wants the original documents and an accounting of how you came to be in possession of them."

"In exchange for what?" asked Jesse, rather aggressively.

"The peace and quiet of your lives back sounds rather attractive, does it not?"

"Are you saying that if we don't agree, we can expect more of the type of activity Alfredo Menendez brought?" asked Greg sharply.

"Not at all," said Cortez smoothly, "I was just observing that your lives have been more placid since Mr. Menendez was arrested this last time."

"You'd be right about that, but we are prepared to fight to keep that peace and quiet now," Susan said fiercely "You could say that we've been far more vigilant and prepared since Alfredo went back to jail and plan to stay that way to preserve our peace and quiet,".

"Mr. McVey doesn't want a fight, he wants a peaceful, mutually acceptable resolution."

"In which he gets what he wants," Jesse added.

"In which he gets what he wants, and you get what you want."

"And what is it we want, Mr. Cortez?" asked Greg, getting down to the nub of the matter.

"Why, money, of course."

"Mr. McVey will pay to shut us up?" Jen asked incredulously.

"In a word, yes."

"I know this sounds crass Mr. Cortez," said Jesse, "but how much?"

"How much is fair? Five hundred dollars each? A thousand? Make me an offer."

"A thousand dollars sounds generous until you consider what Ms. Belle Isle has gone through, not to mention the hours and hours of research we've all been doing to back track this claim. What would Mr. McVey call it? Pain and suffering?" asked Susan.

"Ten thousand each," Jesse suggested.

"That's a lot of pain and suffering, Mr. Grimes, perhaps too much."

"Five thousand," Jen blurted before she knew what she was saying.

"Is that a unanimous offer?" Cortez asked around the room.

There was a slow but definite nodding of heads.

"Very well, I'll take that offer to Mr. McVey. In exchange he'll expect an accounting of how you came to have the documents, the documents themselves and, of course, your silence. If he agrees, I'll bring back a nondisclosure agreement for each of you to sign and five thousand dollars cash each."

Cortez stood up, saying his goodbyes and headed for the door. Greg made it to the door in time to open it for Cortez and he said good night as the man walked out and Greg closed the door behind him.

CHAPTER 24

The two U.S. Marshals secured Alfredo Menendez pretty much the way the jail guards had for Sergeant Salazar's visits, handcuffs and belly chain. They debated using leg irons as well but decided since one of them would be in the back seat with him, they weren't necessary. Both men were armed with sidearms, tasers and pepper spray and had been carefully trained how to use each and under what circumstances. Both were relatively new officers, fresh out of the U.S. Marshal's Training Academy in Glynco, Georgia, and not at all familiar with Tucson. But they were also equipped with GPS so they were confident they could find their way around and locate Sergeant Salazar's targets based on what Alfredo saw and told them.

When they set off, Alfredo told them to head to South Tucson, as that was where most of the targets were. The Marshals had been instructed to take copious notes and photographs if possible but under no circumstances be obvious about their surveillance. The pair were pumped about being entrusted with such a mission but played it down as just another assignment.

Alfredo first showed them McVey's law offices on West 22nd Street and South 10th Avenue. They duly took photographs as they drove by. He then directed them deeper into South Tucson. This was Alfredo's home turf and he knew it backward and forward. When they got close to the Denny's Restaurant on 22nd he started groaning and holding his stomach.

He moaned and said urgently, "Oh man, I gotta take a dump! I think the peppers they gave us last night were spoiled. I gotta go, bad!" This had *not* been covered in the Marshal's training academy or their briefing for this assignment and the driver was near panic-stricken.

"What should we do?" he asked his partner who was every bit as undecided..

"Oh man! I gotta go real bad, can't you stop somewhere?" Alfredo moaned. "I don't think I can hold it much longer." Knowing of the Denny's up 22nd, Alfredo groaned again. I can't wait until we get back to the jail. There's a Denny's a couple of blocks up, can you stop there. Ohh God, hurry!"

The driver spotted the Denny's sign and made a sharp turn into the parking lot. He pulled up to the curb and the back seat Marshal got out then helped Alfredo out. Alfredo bent double and moaned again, louder this time. The escorting Marshal bent to help steady Alfredo, and the prisoner straightened up and slugged the Marshal with a double fist to the temple, knocking him senseless. Alfredo took off toward the back of the restaurant, knowing that beyond it was a maze of alleyways and dead end lanes in which they would never find him.

At first, the driver didn't know what had happened. All he knew was that the prisoner was loose, and his partner was nowhere in sight. He slammed the car in park and leaped out, running around the other side of the car where he found his partner unconscious. He wasn't sure if he should pursue the prisoner or see to his partner but common sense quickly prevailed and he knelt down to check on his companion. Then he thought of the radio and opened the front passenger door to get to the radio microphone. In a panicked voice he called for an ambulance and reported the escape, giving his location and Alfredo's description. In less than ten minutes the area was crawling with Tucson PD cars, but Alfredo, fast as a deer, was long gone into the maze behind Denny's.

He hadn't run more than a few blocks, through back yards and alleys until he came to his best friend's house. Carlos was home, and awake, and helped Alfredo cut through the handcuffs. They wiped the cuffs down then wrapped them in an old newspaper and Alfredo tossed the bundle into a dumpster several blocks away from his friend's house.

Alfredo ran the rest of the way to his own house and was shocked to find it empty and a for rent sign in the window. She was gone! She had taken the children and gone back to Mexico as she had threatened. It was all the fault of that gringa *puta* who kicked him in the head.

Common sense told him to head for Mexico. There was nothing left for him here. If The *federales* caught him, he would die in prison; if Jimbo McVey caught him, he would die earlier but just as dead. But Alfredo was caught up in his machismo *venganza*, his pride required that he exact revenge on the bitch who caused all this . . . preferably with his blade.

He walked into the back yard of his old house and slipped inside through a broken basement window. He went upstairs and found most of their personal possessions gone but she had left his clothes, which he expected. He quickly changed from the orange jail jumpsuit to his regular street clothes then pulled up the trim piece above the closet door. He had widened out the gap in the void between the door frame and the header covered by the trim piece and put hinges on the trim piece so he could have quick access to the void. It was a clever, easily accessible hiding place in which no one ever thought to look. Including his wife. Months ago, he had hidden five hundred dollars in cash, a switchblade knife and a .38 caliber five-shot revolver for just such an emergency. It was all still there and Alfredo stuffed the items in his pockets. He walked back over to Carlos's house and spent the night.

The next morning he had to find some wheels. The cops had undoubtedly towed his old Chevy and the car he had borrowed from the tow company. He'd just have to steal something.

*****

"Twenty thousand dollars to buy them off? That's robbery!"

roared Jimbo McVey.

"They started out wanting ten thousand apiece," said Cortez. "Started talking about pain and suffering and what the one woman went through with the robberies and dug their heels in at five thousand apiece. And no, it would not have been cheaper to have them wasted."

McVey inhaled as if ready to speak then shook his head. He pressed a button on his intercom to his receptionist and said, "Maria, I need four boilerplate non-disclosure agreements, Mr. Cortez will give you the names and details."

"Don't give them a penny until they hand over all the documents and tell you how they got them. I also want to know how they found the claim and if there's documentation, I want that too. Examine the documents carefully. I only have copies so have no way of judging the authenticity of the ones they have. If they're scamming me, that's how we'll know, and if it's a scam, you know what to do."

"I thought you didn't want a messy, high profile investigation."

"I don't, but I can't afford to let someone try to pull one over on me. I don't have any choice. My reputation would be damaged so cost would not be an obstacle."

"If it comes to that, I'll try to make it seem less sensational."

McVey nodded as Cortez left the room.

He called Jen the next morning while the others were at work, and made an appointment to come by the apartment at 6 PM to consummate their deal.

*****

Alfredo almost laughed. It was almost impossibly easy to

steal cars from some people such as the lady dressed in a business suit who had left her BMW running while she ran into the coffee shop to get her latte. Alfredo was in the car and almost out of the parking lot before the woman even placed her order with the barista!

Now that he had wheels, Alfredo's almost smile turned into a grim line as he contemplated his next move. He would lie in wait for the bitch to show near her car then settle with her once and for all, then head to Mexico. If he couldn't reach her before she got to her car, he would shoot her but not kill her. He wanted the pleasure of cutting her throat.

At about 11 AM he drove into the apartment complex on Haughton and spotted Jen's Honda right away. He had to wait until the right space opened up so he could be close enough to strike when she appeared.

When a nearby space he wanted finally opened up, Alfredo settled in to wait. He was not necessarily a patient man, but for her, he had all the time in the world.

Jen and Greg had received word last evening by phone that Alfredo had escaped. She had been assured that her apartment would receive periodic drive bys through the night which was about all the protection Tucson PD could afford to give her considering the latest round of budget cuts. It was an uncomfortable feeling, being there alone in the apartment with just her Smith and Wesson for company.

But she had a 1:30 PM appointment with a gold buyer that she didn't want to miss even though Tucson PD had recommended that she stay home with the doors locked. She had pretty much had all the bullshit she was going to put up with from that idiot and got ready to go to her appointment.

At 1:00 PM, gun in hand, Jen walked out of her apartment and walked toward her car. As she got to the front fender of the vehicle, she heard a car engine rev to life and the squeal of tires. A car roared out of a parking space nearby and came toward her. The driver's window was down and she could see an arm holding what looked like a gun sticking out the window then heard several shots.

Per Greg's contingency instructions, she immediately dropped to the ground, nearly losing her grip on her pistol. The car squealed to a stop and she heard a door open and footsteps running toward her but couldn't yet see anyone.

"Where are you, you bitch?" screamed Alfredo as he advanced. Finally he appeared between her car and the next. He had dropped the now-empty revolver and was coming at her with his switchblade extended before him. Jen didn't hesitate, she opened fire and emptied her the magazine of the Smith into his torso.

It wasn't like in the movies. Alfredo wasn't thrown backward by the impact of Jen's shots, or even collapse to the pavement. He just stopped and the hand holding the knife dropped to his side. There was a surprised look on his face as he slipped down to his knees then fell forward on the pavement.

Jen lay there breathing heavily for a moment as her neighbor ran up to see what the excitement was about. As Jen struggled to her feet, using her car for support, she called to the woman, "Call 911! There's been a shooting and there's a man down." The woman produced a cell phone and turned to make the call.

"You bastard," Jen muttered, "I told you if you came after me again I'd kill you." She watched the blood pooling around Alfredo as it grew bigger and bigger and crept over and under the knife. Suddenly she turned and vomited onto the curb in front of her car.

It seemed like forever but hardly any time at all elapsed before Tucson PD and an ambulance drew up. Once the officers had ascertained that the scene was stable, they allowed the EMTs access to Alfredo. The responding officer who reached her first was businesslike but not cold, as he relieved Jen of her gun and found a place for her to sit down in the front seat of his car.

Soon detectives and technicians swarmed the crime scene

for the investigation. In addition to the knife, the technicians found Alfredo's gun and three bullet holes in Jen's car. Surprisingly, Alfredo's aim had been true and had she remained standing, she would have been shot. There were no witnesses since most everyone was at work but the evidence was telling, and there was never a question that it was a homicide in self-defense.

The investigation was winding down when Greg arrived home from the base. He quickly learned the circumstances and went in search of Jen. He found her seated in the Watch Commander's front seat with the door open. When she saw him she looked askance at the lieutenant who nodded. She climbed out of the car and went straight into his arms where she stayed for several long minutes.

Finally, the officers turned her loose and she and Greg walked down to their apartment. Once inside, Greg asked her if she wanted a drink but she passed, opting for a cold bottle of water. They sat down on the couch and Greg asked her if she wanted to talk.

She shook her head, "Everything that needed to be said has been said." But she snuggled into his side and remained there until Jesse and Susan showed up. She told them about their imminent appointment with Lester Cortez.

CHAPTER 25

Cortez was at the apartment door promptly at 6 PM and his knock was again answered by Greg who indicated that the fixer should sit in the same chair. This time Cortez was dressed in slacks, pullover v-necked sweater and button-down shirt. He looked more like a businessman than an enforcer. First, he handed around the non-disclosure agreements, allowed the four friends to read them thoroughly then solicited questions. None were forthcoming.

"Understand that if you violate this agreement, Mr. McVey would use the courts to ruin you both financially and leave your reputations in tatters. *If you live that long.* Be sure you can forever remain silent before you sign these, they carry a lot of weight both in civil and criminal court."

That caused the foursome to read them again then look questions at each other. Finally, Greg spoke up, "This only applies to the Cactus Wren claim, nothing else, right?"

"That's right. I just wanted to make sure you understood how restricting this is when the subject of the claim comes up."

"Okay," said Greg, "I'm good with that." He thereupon signed his name to both copies and gave one back to Cortez. The others followed and Cortez tucked the documents back in the briefcase.

"Now, you have some documents for me?"

"I assume everything but the letter is a copy," said Greg These are the actual documents I found, and I'm sure the letter and its envelope are original. Feel free to look them over carefully."

You'll never know how carefully I'll look these documents over, son, your life depends on it.

Cortez concentrated on the letter from Albert Neal until he was satisfied it was the real thing. He had to look closely; McVey would scrutinize it even closer. Even the copies looked like carbon copies from the original document; there was no copy machine involved.

"They look fine. Now you have a story to tell, right? Let me set up a recorder so Mr. McVey can hear it for himself."

Greg launched into the story of ejecting from his aircraft, landing, injuring his knee and seeking shelter in the cave. He told how he found the saddlebags and the papers inside and how he didn't even read them until just before he was rescued. He told how he entrusted them to the Pararescueman until he was released from the hospital after his surgery and how he recovered them from the same man.

"What became of the wallet you found and the saddlebags?" asked Cortez.

"I don't know, I left them in the cave and I don't think the helo crew had time to retrieve them so they're probably still there."

"Do you think the Pararescueman could have taken a look at these documents, say, after he gave you a shot?"

"I'd be very surprised. He was concentrating pretty much on my knee, besides, he put them in a self-sealing personal possessions bag and I initialed across the seal. It was still intact when Jesse and I got them back."

"How did you find the claim?"

"We scoured the internet for any trace of Ahren's Seep but found nothing. Jen even went to Yuma researching the names on the claim application. She found some of their names but nothing that gave her a clue where the claim was. I finally found Ahren's seep on an old Arizona Territorial map dated before the letter was written by Albert Neal. It was a metes and bounds description on the claim application so we took an educated guess that the Ahren's Seep had been dug or drilled out into a well that came to be known as Charlie Bell Well. We went to the well, found the claim's landmarks, laid out the boundaries described in the claim application then began searching for the cache of equipment and supplies which we found with the help of a metal detector."

"What became of that map?" asked Cortez.

"It's right here along with copies of all our computer searches and the map I drew showing the location of the claim and the cache of equipment and supplies."

"Although it isn't a specific part of our agreement, I'm sure Mr. McVey would like to see them."

"He can have them, they're of no use to us anymore," said Greg.

"Do you have anything else connected to the Cactus Wren claim?"

No one was going to fess up to ownership of the two nuggets or the gold so the unanimous answer was no.

"If there's nothing else, I guess we're through," said Cortez, looking carefully at the four people before him as he handed out packets of fifty hundred-dollar bills. Cortez was satisfied it was a clean transaction. He detected more than a little tension in the foursome but no tells suggesting subterfuge.

He hoped McVey would settle for the results. He drove back to the lawyer's office and delivered the recording and the documents. Before dismissing him, McVey insisted on listening to the recording twice and carefully examining the documents with a magnifying glass. Finally he was satisfied.

"If you ever hear that Alfredo Menendez is on the street, let me know, I owe him.

Better yet bring him to me."

*****

After Cortez left, Greg looked at his friends with his arms spread wide and his hands spread outward. "I don't know whether to be afraid the other shoe will drop or laugh out loud."

"By damn, *I* know what to do," said Jesse as he jumped up

and went into the kitchen, emerging moments later with four glasses and a bottle of champagne. "I've been saving this for months for a special occasion and I reckon this qualifies. Not only do we have the mobster off our back and a fortune in gold, but five thousand dollars each walking around money."

That broke the ice and everyone started talking at once as Jesse opened the bottle and filled each glass. He raised his and said, "To Jimbo McVey, I wish him luck." Everyone raised a glass and said, "Here here."

Susan said, "I want a closer look at one of those bottles, can we take one out of one of the packs just to look at it, and maybe weigh it on the bathroom scale?"

Greg obligingly got up and, using both hands, retrieved one of the bottles of gold from the bedroom. Jen had spread a newspaper on the coffee table and put the bathroom scale on it. Greg put the bottle down on it. The digital scale read thirty-two pounds and change.

"No wonder that pack was so heavy going up the pass!" Jesse exclaimed.

"There's about thirty-one grams in a troy ounce," said Jen, her calculator out. "And Fourteen point six troy ounces in a pound, times thirty-two equals four hundred sixty-seven troy ounces. Gold is at about eighteen hundred dollars a troy ounce, so multiplying the two is $840,960. Jesse, you were carrying about two and a half million dollars on your back both times you hiked up the pass. Greg carried the same number of bottles so that doubles the figure to ten million plus the three point three million Susan and I were carrying. That adds up to over thirteen million dollars at today's gold prices."

Everyone including Jen was stunned into silence. Almost as an afterthought, Jen said, "That's three and a quarter million apiece." They all stared at the gold as if it was a genie in the bottle.

It wasn't much to look at, just a dusty old fifth of whiskey bottle, mostly clear in color, with air bubbles throughout and thousands of particles of gold staring back at them.

EPILOGUE

By the time the federal, state and local revenue agencies were done with them, the Cactus Wren Claim gang got to keep just over fifty-three percent of what they had found. That was roughly a million and a half bucks each, but none of them felt the need to quit working and live the "easy" life. Both men loved to fly and knew that at some point, when their flying days were behind them, they would revisit the concept of living the good life.

Susan was not as enamored of her career in the Air Force. It wasn't that she hated her work, as much as she saw nothing but more administrative assignments in her future there. Secretly, she would love to resign her commission and just have a couple of babies with Jesse.

Jen was the one in a quandary. She too didn't mind what she was doing though it was boring beyond words at times. She seriously considered going back to school but had no more of an idea what to study than she did at eighteen right out of high school, and she already had two degrees. She had all but decided to go into real estate and rental management, now that she had a nest egg to fall back on. Her future with Greg wasn't clear, though she would marry him tomorrow if he asked.

All in all, the future looked bright for the foursome.

Jimbo McVey never learned that he had been swindled – by a bunch of amateurs no less. Everyone involved knew the outcome if he ever found out, but the foursome abided by their non-disclosure agreements and never said a word. After six months of unsuccessfully trying to legally get permission to mine the site, McVey secretly started a crew mining the claim and they labored for six more months with little or no payoff before McVey called a halt after deciding someone had already worked the claim between the time of the original claimants and the present. It was a $20,000 investment plus expenses that just didn't pay off.

McVey wound up with other things to worry about since Tucson PD's Sergeant Bud Salazar now had his teeth into him. The "intelligence" provided by Alfredo Menendez was rendered moot by his death, but Salazar finally had a place to start and he *wanted* Jimbo McVey. Salazar was to be disappointed when one of McVey's thugs shot the lawyer to death two years later. No one with any leadership ability stepped forward and Jimbo McVey's organization eventually scattered to the winds.

Lester Cortez never said anything either even though he never learned about the gold. He felt it was a great joke on the big man, and would chuckle about it every time it came to mind. He retired from the "business" one contract later when it went sour and he was almost shot by his target. He retired to the Bahamas where he opened a dive shop, outfitted a dive boat and started searching for a treasure of his own.

Terry L. Shaffer grew up near Oregon City, about twenty miles south of Portland, Oregon. He graduated from Oregon City High School and Clackamas Community College before moving on to Portland State University, majoring in Political Science. Between high school and college, Terry spent four years in the United States Navy, and was assigned duty stations in Long Beach, California, and Naval Intelligence billets in Washington, D.C. and Alameda, California, from where he sailed to the Western Pacific aboard an aircraft carrier and earned both the Vietnam Service Medal and the Vietnam Campaign Medal.

During his college days at Portland State, Terry joined the Clackamas County Sheriff's Department where he was assigned a variety of positions including patrol, detectives and narcotics. He retired in 2000 after twenty-five years' service. After writing thousands of pages of police reports and search warrant affidavits, he likes to say that he has twenty-five years' experience writing in the true crime genre.

Terry began his writing career in fiction shortly before he retired and has been at it ever since. He lives full time in his motor home with his rescue dog-of-many-breeds, Ellie Mae, and divides his time between his home in Colton, Oregon, and various locations in the American Southwest where he spends his time writing and exploring. Terry enjoys off-roading, photography, reading and, of course, writing.

He welcomes feedback and may be reached at jbugley@gmail.com.

Other books by Terry L Shaffer

Legacy of a Primitive

Treachery Island

Caballo Gold

Coronado's Deceit

*Charlie Perkins

*Charlie Perkins: Challenges

*Charlie Perkins: Resolutions

*Charlie Perkins: Conclusions

*Read better as a series than as stand-alones

Made in the USA
Columbia, SC
16 November 2021